I0738451

BOOTS AND MISTLETOE

COWBOY CHRISTMAS, THE MISTLETOE COLLECTION BOOK ONE

EDITH MACKENZIE

This is a work of fiction. Names, **characters**, businesses, places, events, locales, and incidents are either the products of the author's imagination or used in a fictitious manner. Any resemblance to actual persons, living or dead, or actual events is purely coincidental

Boots & Mistletoe (Cowboy Christmas, The Mistletoe Collection Book #1):

Images © DepositPhotos – gpointstudio, re_bekka & PetarPaunchev

Cover Design © Designed with Grace

❊ Created with Vellum

For all those that still believe

A COUPLE WEEKS BEFORE
CHRISTMAS, BRISBANE, AUSTRALIA

The sun beat down overhead, the air thick and humid. On the horizon, dark clouds rolled in ominously, heralding a storm in the not-too-distant future. Jackson was a million miles away from the snowy landscape of his Colorado home—a million miles and about to hold a koala. He looked over at Luciano, his travel companion and fellow United States Representative for the invitation bull ride that was set to be held the next day. The dark-haired Brazilian looked like a little kid on Christmas morning as he enthusiastically took pictures to send back home to his kids. To be fair, it was only a couple of weeks till Christmas, so maybe Luciano had it right to be so excited.

Jackson lifted his buff-colored Stetson to wipe his brow, sticky with sweat. The faint hint of a breeze provided a slight relief from the suspicion that his brain was slowly boiling. He sure as heck wished someone would get this photoshoot started and soon. Jackson had been a professional bull rider long enough to know that publicity shoots were part and parcel of the job, but it had been a long flight from the States to Brisbane, Australia, and his weary, aching body cried out for a long soak in a hot tub.

"My boy and girl, they will be so jealous that I get to hold a real-life koala bear." Luciano handed him a bottle of water, the sides covered in beaded condensation that ran down in rivulets. "Frankie, my wife, she is always talking about drop bears, but I asked the handler and he says they're too dangerous to have on display." Luciano scratched his chin. "She was very clear before I left that she wanted a photo of me with one."

Jackson shrugged. "Maybe sneak a koala in your suitcase for Christmas and she'll forget all about the drop bear?"

Luciano's eyes lit up as he laughed. "The twins, they would think I was the best papai if I did that. I do not think I want the responsibility of caring for one."

The Brazilian stopped talking as a blonde woman approached. "Hi, I'm Kelly." She extended her hand first to Luciano and then to Jackson. He was pleasantly surprised at her firm grip and direct eye contact, some of his irritation disappearing now that it looked as though they were going to get started. "I apologize for the delay, but I'm hopeful we can get started soon." She glanced at the water bottles they both held. "Can I get either of you any more water? Something to eat?" Both men shook their heads. "Okay. Well, I'll leave you guys to it and, fingers crossed, we'll get this show on the road soon."

Jackson did his best to smother the frustrated sigh that escaped him. This was turning out to be like *The NeverEnding Story.* He wistfully thought about the tub waiting for him back at his hotel room. A short distance away, he could hear Kelly muttering on the phone about someone not showing up and that she needed whomever she was speaking to to come out. Jackson shook his head at the debacle and looked around for a place to sit in the shade. Finding one under a large tree, he settled down, stretching his legs out and crossing them comfortably at the ankles, arms folded across his broad chest. If this went on long enough, he might even have time for a nap.

Alas, it was not to last, and after ten minutes or so of respite from the sun, a sleek Mercedes pulled up. Curiously, he watched as the door opened and a woman stepped out. He felt like he'd been hit by a sledgehammer, the breath rushing out of him. The woman in question had long sandy-brown hair that reached midway down her back. From where he sat, he admired it as the sun transformed it into ribbons of honey and caramel. Most of her face was shaded by large, oversized black sunglasses, but he could see her lips were lush and full, her figure slender but curved in all the right places. Looking like she meant business, environmentally-friendly coffee cup in hand, she strode over to Kelly.

"You owe me big time." Her voice had the unmistakable Aussie accent, but it was somehow smoother. "You know how Lance gets."

"Yeah, well, your boyfriend can bloody get over it. This is business and your job, and I need your help." Kelly looked over to the cowboys and, seeing that they were being watched, beckoned the stranger to follow her. "Luciano, Jackson, this is my friend and colleague, Quinn."

Quinn. Her name whispered through him as if, somehow, he should have known. He blinked, aware that she had her hand extended, waiting for him to accept. He reached out, his hand suddenly feeling coarse against her soft one.

"Pleased to meet you, ma'am"

She smiled, those full lips curving upwards. He wished he could see her eyes, but they remained a mystery to him, still hidden behind her sunglasses. "I believe that is the first time I've ever been called ma'am."

"Better than a lot of other things he could have called you," ribbed Kelly.

Those lips curved upwards even more, exposing straight white teeth. "That's true. And in this game, we've heard them all."

Kelly took Quinn by the arm. "If you blokes will excuse us, Quinn needs to get changed. She's graciously agreed to step in to be the promotional girl for this shoot at the last minute." Quinn's brows quirked upwards, silently signaling her thoughts on the matter.

Jackson couldn't contain the pleased smile that tugged at his lips. The day was definitely improving. He watched as the women left, his gaze riveted to Quinn's departing form, admiring the gentle sweep of her curves.

"I remember how my world was rocked when I met my Querida, my wife, Frankie." Luciano's eyes sparkled, a knowing look on his face.

"I'm just enjoying the view."

"That's how it always starts and then BAM!" Luciano clapped his hands together to emphasize his point. "Before you know it, you're a goner." Jackson didn't even dignify his friend's comment with a response, instead tracking Quinn's progress until she disappeared from view, stoically trying to ignore the Brazilian's mocking laughter.

QUINN PULLED the jeans up over her slim hips, zipping them, her thoughts winging back to the handsome cowboy she'd just been introduced to. When Kelly had called her to beg and then demand she come out and model for the promo shoot, she'd expected some grizzled and scarred bull riders, their bodies bent from their profession. Not the virile tall cowboy, Jackson Gregory, with his raw spellbinding masculinity.

It had been all she'd been able to manage not to simper up at him as he'd stared intently at her with his piecing blue eyes. Eyes that were only slightly less blue than the summer sky above them. Sure, with his golden sun-kissed skin and a body that seemed to be made of hard muscle and sinew, he was undoubtedly an extremely attractive man.

But it had been his smile—broad and a little bashful like he knew the impact he had on women and was ever so slightly embarrassed and apologetic about it. It was the countenance of a nice guy, and it took her breath away. At the same time, she'd found herself hesitantly smiling back. Honestly, it had been impossible not to.

She pulled the logo-emblazoned, incredibly tight-fitting midriff T-shirt over her head, beginning to regret the extra piece of Vegemite toast she'd had for breakfast. Quinn looked down at herself, already knowing it was an outfit her boyfriend, Lance, would not approve of her wearing without him, let alone for a promotional photoshoot with cowboys that included an extraordinarily attractive one. She shook her head to dispel Jackson's breathtaking image from her mind.

"Are you almost ready in there?" Kelly called from outside.

"Just need to do my hair and makeup." Quinn began to pull some products from the oversized bag she always carried. It was lucky for Kelly that she always came prepared. A girl never knew when she might need to freshen up.

Kelly opened the door. "Sit down. I'll do that for you." Obediently, Quinn complied, turning her face so her friend could touch up her face. "I do appreciate you doing this for me, you know."

"I know. I just wish it wasn't going to be such a drama

with Lance. I swear he's getting worse, not better. It's like he's just waiting for an opportunity to tell me how much of a disappointment I am, that I didn't live up to his expectations."

Quinn couldn't remember when Lance had started to change. Except for a high-school crush, he'd been her first serious boyfriend and she'd been flattered when the older, accomplished property developer had shown interest in her at a corporate event. He'd introduced her to a glamourous side of life that she'd only previously glimpsed, far removed from her solidly working-class upbringing. Now that she thought about it, he'd changed once she'd finished her degree and started working with Kelly. Or maybe it was her who had changed, wanting to prove herself on her own merits, not as his arm candy.

Oblivious to her friend's somber thoughts, Kelly began to apply a coat of bright scarlet to Quinn's lips. "If I'd known bull riders were so bloody cute, I'd have started going to rodeos years ago." Kelly pretended to fan herself. "I don't ever think I've seen a man who, well, is such a hunk of pure gorgeousness as that Jackson Gregory." It was hard to disagree. The good Lord knew he'd made an impact on her. "The other one, Luciano, he's such a sweetheart. All he can talk about is his wife and kids. She's an Aussie, but I think it's the first time he's been here. I think he's actually missing them."

Quinn had barely noticed the other bull rider—only dimly aware of him—when they'd been introduced. Kelly stood back to admire her handywork. "I think this is going to work out much better than with the girl we'd originally booked. You're much prettier."

"And cheaper."

"That too." Kelly started putting Quinn's makeup back in her bag and then grabbed a hairbrush, smoothing out her long dark honey-colored tresses. "Now, let's go out and get this shoot started. I think we've made the hot cowboys wait long enough."

Quinn took a final look at herself and followed Kelly out into the bright sun. The two bull riders stood with the animal handlers, petting the pair of koalas they held. Kelly made another fanning motion with her hand. As if he could feel her gaze on him, the tall cowboy turned his head, his eyes locking with Quinn's. She felt a shiver dance up her spine. She mentally chastised herself. *You're being ridiculous. Now stop this and be a professional.*

"Quinn, I want you to stand in the middle and hold one of the koalas, and then one of you guys on each side," Kelly directed. Quinn was surprised at the weight of the animal and the faint fragrance of eucalyptus as she took up her position.

"My Querida will be so jealous that I get to pet a koala," Luciano said, smiling as he posed, stroking the animal.

"Kelly said something about your wife being an Aussie?" Quinn said, overly aware of Jackson's hard body on her other side.

"Yes, I fear that she will be a bit disappointed that I did not get a photo with a drop bear, but the keepers have informed me it is for my own safety." Luciano sighed melodramatically. "I had wished to put it in her Christmas stocking as a little surprise."

"Maybe you can slip something else as a little surprise in her stocking," Jackson said, blue eyes twinkling with mischievous innocence as he waggled his brows.

Quinn let out a splutter, not sure what to address first. She turned slightly at the photographer's direction to change the angle. She decided it might be best to ignore Jackson's comment and focus on Luciano's. "Um, drop bear?"

"Yes, a relative of the koala that has big fangs"—he held

his fingers up to his mouth to mimic the deadly beast—"and drops on its prey from trees. Have you never seen one?"

"They're pretty rare. You have about as much of a chance of seeing one as a hoop snake."

Quinn shifted the koala in her arms, the creature beginning to get heavy. Jackson placed his hand beneath hers, helping to support the animal. Quinn could feel his calloused palm, the skin rough on the back of her hand. Trying to take her focus off the sensation, she returned her attention back to Luciano.

"Have you bought any gifts for your family since you've been here?"

"We only arrived yesterday," Jackson answered for his friend. "I have to say, it doesn't feel like Christmas here."

"What do you mean? There are Christmas trees up everywhere," argued Quinn, defensive over what she perceived as a slight to her country's Christmas spirit.

Jackson's thumb rubbed her hand in a slow circular motion as if he was gentling a fractious horse. "I didn't mean anything by it. But I've never had a Christmas that didn't involve a good few feet of snow."

Quinn laughed, suddenly understanding. "It's not Christmas here if it's not hot. I mean, most people head to the beach."

Jackson shook his head in amazement. "Back home, it's all about eggnog and cocoa, snow, fires crackling, family." His face softened as he spoke. It was clear this cowboy had a fond spot for the festive season.

"Well, here, it's all about the seafood and backyard cricket —and family, of course." Quinn held the koala out to the keeper who had come over to collect it. "At heart, it's the same holiday. Or as my dad would say, same meat, different gravy. It's just the trimming that's different."

Jackson laughed at her terminology. "Does Frankie talk

like this all the time, too?"

Luciano shook his head fondly. "When I first met Frankie, I never felt like I understood the words coming from her mouth. But my heart understood, and that was all that mattered." He flicked a suggestive look between the two of them.

Quinn felt herself blush, uncomfortable that he might be implying something that wasn't true. "Well, my boyfriend is Australian, so he doesn't have that problem." Was it her imagination or did Jackson look disappointed at her revelation? Kelly, having just made her way over, rolled her eyes, making a face at the mention of Lance. Could her friend be any more obvious about her lack of regard for Quinn's boyfriend?

"Thanks for saving the day, Quinn. You were great," Kelly complemented. "And thank you both for your patience while we sorted everything out. I'll forward copies of the media release to your manager," she continued, addressing the cowboys.

"It was my pleasure, ma'am," Jackson said, sending a warm look to Quinn. Kelly's eyes opened dramatically wide as she caught the gaze. "Will you be at the bull ride?"

Quinn tried to ignore her friend's encouraging nod. "Um, I have plans, but it sounds like it will be a good night out."

"I'll be there working," Kelly said to her. "You should come and keep me company."

"Maybe I'll come down and check it out if anything changes," Quinn said non-committedly. What was Kelly trying to do? She had a boyfriend.

Jackson flashed a winning smile at her, his eyes capturing her own. Seriously, the man had the most unbelievable presence. "Make sure you come and say hello if you do. I would like to see you again."

The problem was, Quinn wanted to see him again, too.

CHAPTER 2

The slow blink of the cursor on the computer screen was in danger of hypnotizing Quinn. Frustrated, she rubbed her eyes. *How hard was it to get talent that actually showed up?* At this rate, she would never get the next week of promotions scheduled. The sharp chime of her phone pulled her attention away from her dilemma. Lance's name flashed up with a message. He was canceling dinner plans in favor of going out for drinks with clients.

When no sting of disappointment came, she realized she was relieved. It saddened her that her relationship had come to a point where not having to spend time with her boyfriend, to be spared the humiliation of being corrected and belittled for how she acted or spoke or dressed, made her breathe in deeply, luxuriating in a sense of respite. She wondered if maybe he would tire of her soon, maybe replace her with a younger, more easily malleable model since he no longer felt the need to show her off anymore.

Her thoughts turned morose. Where had all the fun in her life gone? She was too young to feel this bitter, used up and spent. Quinn's mind conjured up an image of laughing, teasing blue eyes in a handsome tanned face. Making her decision, she grabbed her handbag. To heck with it all! She was going to have some fun. Looks like she was going to a rodeo after all.

Quinn couldn't recall a time she'd ever seen a venue overflowing with so many RM Williams boots and Akubra hats. Self-consciously, she clutched her designer logo-emblazoned bag, aware that no one else was wearing ripped jeans. Ripped *designer* jeans, she corrected herself. *And they made my bum look great, thank you very much.* That, and the heels helped. With a definite flick of her head, she marched inside.

On her way to her seat, a cowgirl sashayed past, her sparkly, rhinestone-studded belt inducing such a state of envy that, for a moment, Quinn had to pause to appreciate it. "That belt is everything."

The girl flicked her a smile. "Thanks. Love your jeans."

Quinn finally located her seat and looked around curiously. It seemed that the drink of choice for most of the spectators was rum drunk straight from black cans. The air was sickly sweet with the smell of it. She'd helped Kelly with a few events in this venue. It always amazed her how a location could be completely changed for whatever was required given the individual nature of that particular event. Out in the center of the stadium, the usual flooring had been covered in sand to give the bulls grip or maybe for the bull riders to bounce, she assumed. She wasn't entirely sure, but a spark of an idea hit her. She knew someone that did.

Quickly, she dug her phone out of her bag, impatiently waiting for it to be answered.

"Hey, Kelly, whereabouts are you?"

"Quinn? Geeze it's noisy where you are. Hang on a minute, are you here? At the rodeo?" There were random noises coming down the line. Quinn couldn't be certain, but it sounded like someone trying to break out of jail.

"Yeah, Lance bailed on me and I thought this might be more fun than sitting at home alone on a Friday night."

"Head to the back and I'll meet you at the side door. You can come on back here."

Quinn didn't need to be asked twice. She stood, shuffling and slipping pass spectators who were trying to find their seats. Cowboys giving her the once-over and suggestive looks, girls throwing her dirty glares when they saw the attention she was receiving from the men that they wanted to be on the receiving end of. As she got closer to the access door, the pungent aroma of livestock made her wrinkle her nose against its assault on her senses.

"Hey, chick." Kelly waved her over, hanging an access lanyard around her neck and ushering her through the door. Backstage was a cacophony of sights and sounds. Official looking older men in black shirts, big hats and clipboards were deep in conversation. Further along, a group of paramedics in their bottle-green jumpsuits casually lounged against the wall and on chairs, a large first aid kit and stretcher at the ready. Quinn shuddered as she envisioned some of the gory injuries that might need to be treated tonight.

Quinn jumped when a gate clanged shut, bulls moving restlessly as they were moved into position, the stock contractors yelling and jostling them about. A nearby cowboy smirked at her. "Honey, if you jump on my lap, I'll make sure those mean old bulls don't get to you." His friends beside him laughed at his attempt at humor.

"I'd rather take my chances with the bulls, thanks," Quinn tartly replied, barely breaking stride as she raised her chin disdainfully.

"She'd probably ride it better than you, too, Dave," his friend ribbed him, giving him a none-too-gentle shove.

"Yeah, she looks like she's good for at least eight seconds."

The group laughed raucously, reminding her of kookaburras on a powerline and with about as much intelligence as galahs.

Quinn could feel the slow burn of anger roll up through her at their comments. Kelly grabbed her arm and forced her to continue forward. "I can see the steam coming out of your ears, but seriously, they're just disrespectful jerks and the world is full of them. If you stop to ream them out every time your path crossed with one, you'd never get anything done."

She followed her friend's lead, disappointment leaving a bitter taste in her mouth until she could take it no longer. "You're wrong. They should be pulled up on talking to a woman like that."

Kelly stopped, crossing her arms across her chest, her mouth downturned. "Like how you pull Lance up every time he treats you like you're nothing but a pretty face and some boobs in front of his friends, or worse, in front of his clients? I'm all for you having some backbone and standing up for women, but maybe start with your boyfriend first."

Quinn chewed the inside of her mouth. She wanted to set her friend straight, rail against the injustice of her words. The only problem? Kelly was right, she was a coward and a hypocrite, and she knew it.

THE SOUND of leather against rope and cowboys hiding nerves behind banter mingled with the smell of rosin and livestock in the melting pot behind the chutes of the rodeo. Jackson breathed in deeply as he mentally began to prepare himself for the ultimate competition of man against beast, perspiration from the humid air making his shirt stick to his skin. He watched as Luciano made his way over.

"I didn't think you were ever going to get off the phone. I

was worried I'd have to tell the stewards that you'd changed your mind, too scared of the Australian bulls," Jackson greeted him.

"Luciano Jnr and Harper wanted to Facetime. They had lots to say, but still not many words I could understand."

Luciano smiled fondly as he spoke of his twin children. Jackson felt a stab of envy snake through him. The Brazilian had been at the top of his game for the better part of a decade. He had a beautiful, loving wife who was also a champion in her own right, and twin children he adored. To cap it off, he was also a generous, loyal friend to those he cared about and one of the nicest people you'd ever meet. It made Jackson feel like he was an underachiever.

"Be careful tonight, my friend," Luciano said, pulling his protection vest from his gear bag. "The style of bulls here are smaller than back home, but still you have to ride them well. They are very nimble, quick on their feet and whippy." He stopped talking, looking around, perplexed at the buzz in the room. There was an energy amongst the competitors that was different to what usually flowed behind the chutes.

Jackson looked around, trying to trace the origin too. He could see heads whipping about, cowboys whispering, commenting to their compatriots, and then he saw her. Jackson had thought that his response to meeting her was an initial reaction, one that would be dulled if he was ever to see her again. Instead, awareness slammed into his ribcage, making him hyperaware of her presence. Anchoring his hands on his belt, he watched her slow approach, appreciating the way the torn denim jeans accentuated every curve, the heels giving her a strut that would make a supermodel proud. The way she smiled at him made him feel invincible, ready to conquer the bull he'd been matched to and not even break a sweat.

"Hi, you made it." Jackson wanted to kick himself for the

stupid comment. Obviously she'd made it. She was here, standing right in front of him. Those gorgeous lips of hers curved as her smile broadened. Jackson forced himself to keep breathing as he stared into her eyes, noticing the green flecked through the hazel.

"I did, and it's already been quite an experience—and no one's even ridden a bull yet," Quinn said, looking past him to smile at Luciano. "Hello, I have something for you." She reached into her bag and pulled out a little stuffed kangaroo and crocodile. "I know they're not much, but I thought your kids might like them." Quinn bit her lip, as though amused, and reached into her bag a second time. Jackson leaned forward when he heard Kelly's snort of derision. In Quinn's other hand was a stuffed koala, a pair of paper fangs attached to its mouth. "It's the best I could come up with, but maybe you can put this in your wife's Christmas stocking. I'm sure she'll get a kick out of it."

Jackson couldn't quite put his finger on it, but it felt like there might be more to the gift than met the eye. "How did your boyfriend take the news of your photoshoot?"

Quinn gave a little dismissive sniff, shrugging her shoulders non-committedly. Clearly, she did not wish to go into details. Before he could ponder her reaction, a steward began to marshal the competitors in preparation for the opening ceremony.

"Quinn, you don't want to miss this, it's going to be spectacular. Like, I mean fireworks, and they're going to set fire to the sand in the arena and have the cowboys step through it as they are introduced," Kelly said, excitement shading her expression as she gave little enthused claps in anticipation.

"I'd better get back to my seat so I don't miss a thing. Good luck to both of you." Quinn turned to depart.

Jackson felt his stomach clench at the thought of her leaving. "Are you coming to the afterparty?"

White teeth bit indecisively on her plump bottom lip. "There's an afterparty?" The words hung in the air for a moment. "Well, when in Rome, or at a rodeo as the case may be." And with a cheeky wink, she walked away, leaving him to, as what was quickly becoming a habit, admire the view as she departed.

A sense of steely resolve filled him. This woman, Quinn, was going to be out there somewhere in the stands as he rode, as he fought for supremacy against a raging bull for eight seconds. Suddenly it was deadly important to him that she think well of him, that she was impressed by his prowess and skill. This woman who had a boyfriend. Not wishing to ponder the feeling too deeply, he gathered his protection vest and stood with the others. If he pursued it too much, he would be forced to admit that it mattered a great deal to him.

CHAPTER 3

Quinn pulled her legs in and smiled politely as a family walked between her and the seats in front, finding their place in the vacant chairs to her left. They took their position with only seconds to spare as the lights were dimmed and spotlights began to cast roving circles on the sand below. An expectant hush fell over the crowd, the announcer beginning to warm the masses up with what was to come next, and then sudden booming explosions made Quinn jump as the fireworks started, tall towers of white, yellow and orange sparks shooting up into the air, a great cloud of smoke wafting to the rafters.

The girl beside her laughed. "I think I almost leapt out of my seat, too."

Quinn shook her head, eyes wide in disbelief. "I wasn't expecting it to be so loud." Out in the center of the arena, the sand had been lit, turning the surface into a lake of lava. One at a time, the cowboys stepped through, chaps flaring with each step they proudly took, hats firmly in place. It was quite the spectacle. Finding herself leaning forward, Quinn forced herself back against her seat.

Her new-found friend beside her sent her an amused glance. "First rodeo?"

Quinn's lips quirked at her green-horn status being so plainly evident. "Yeah. That obvious?"

"Well, I don't think I've ever seen someone with a designer handbag at one before."

Guilty, she looked down at the object in question. Out in the center, the announcer had begun to gee the crowd up for the final two competitors. "Tonight, all the way from the U-S of A, the final event these bull riders will be doing before they get to spend a richly deserved break at home with their loved ones for Christmas. But first, let's see if we can't send them home with a little extra for their troubles. Reigning world champion, Luciano Navarro, and Rookie of the year in his debut season a few years back, finishing top five in the rankings this year, ladies and gentlemen, put your hands together for Jackson Gregory."

Even from high up in the stands, Jackson's presence was unmistakable. He stood head and shoulders above fellow competitors, a giant amongst bull riders.

"Oh my, that is one tall drink of water," the girl beside Quinn muttered. She had to agree.

"Better hope he can run fast. Ain't a bull alive that would miss a target that big," the older man Quinn assumed was the girl's father added.

Quinn jerked her gaze to him in alarm. She hadn't even thought about the possibility of the tall Colorado cowboy getting hurt. Sure, she wasn't stupid. It was bull riding after all, not exactly the safest of professions. It was just that Jackson gave off such an air of quiet competence.

Once the event kicked off, it went surprisingly fast. Quinn was fully invested from the very first ride, oohing and ahhing with the rest of the crowd. Her new friends helpfully explained the finer details, like when one bull rider was penalized for slapping the bull's shoulder with his free hand, or when another was offered a do-over when his bovine failed to perform. Quinn looked down, amused to discover the creases on the denim at her thighs where she'd gripped the fabric tightly with each battle that was fought out on the sand. She was surprised at just how much she was enjoying herself.

She sat a little straighter in her seat when the announcer called that the next competitor to come out of the chute would be one Jackson Gregory. Her heart rate accelerated as the cowboy in charge of opening the gate stood, legs splayed as he gripped the rope firmly, waiting for the nod from Jackson that he was ready. Quinn gave a little gasp as the bull thrashed in the chute, setting the rails to rattling and then, just as she took a breath, the gate was thrown open and the bull plunged out onto the sand, defiance stamped all over his sinewy physique. Jackson looked almost comically big for the bovine. Quickly, Quinn came to perceive that it was a hindrance, not a help.

His broad shoulders and chest sat high above the back of the angry animal, shifting his center of gravity up rather than down low. The bull's smaller size made him agile. He twisted and spun, pivoted and bucked, and all the time, Jackson followed the movement. Quinn held her breath, the denim clasped in her hands damp from the perspiration from her palms, and then the buzzer sounded and, as gracefully as any dancer, he stepped off the bull and bolted madly across the sand to the safety of the arena rails.

Jackson glanced up as he nimbly dropped to the sand once the plunging beast had exited the arena. His score flashed and disappointment flickered across his face. He'd missed out on the win by 0.1 of a point. Humbly, he smiled and waved to the crowd as they went wild at the news that an Aussie cowboy had beaten the Americans and taken home the winner's buckle.

Her friends beside her celebrated, toasting each other with their black cans as Quinn gathered up her bag. It had been one of the most entertaining nights she'd had for quite some time and it hadn't been at all how she'd imagined it. She did feel a teeny bit disappointed for Jackson that he hadn't pulled off the win, but second place wasn't something to be sneezed at either. In fact, the American cowboys had managed to secure second and third place. She bid her companions goodbye and stood to join the queue that had already began to form to exit the building. Quinn had an afterparty to attend.

The bar area that was attached to the sports arena was much more crowded than Quinn had anticipated. In her mind, it was going to be a couple of big hat-wearing cowboys, shooting the breeze over a nice cold beverage. Instead it was a seething mass of people. Fans mingled with the competitors and quite a few women in tight low-cut tops gathered in groups around their favorite bull rider.

Quinn stood on her tiptoes and scanned the crowd to find Kelly and feeling desperately out of place. She was beginning to give serious consideration to leaving when a warm hand touched her arm. She turned to find Luciano standing at her side.

"Quinn, are you lost? I have just returned from calling my Querida to tell her that I was lucky tonight and finished in the places. I am about to find Jackson. I hope he is where I left him and has not wondered off."

She smiled at the image of Jackson being told to stay. "I was looking for Kelly, but I can't seem to find her."

Luciano smiled at her. There was something about him, a warmth that was irresistible. Quinn wasn't sure there was a person alive who wouldn't smile back at this friendly Brazilian. "Maybe we should go find our friends together?"

Quinn nodded. It was better than standing like a shag on a rock looking like a loser. Plus, she genuinely enjoyed listening to Luciano talk about his wife and kids. It was refreshing after the talk of the guys who Lance always had around.

"Ahh," Luciano said in a pleased tone as they made their way through the throng of people. "There is something to be said for having tall friends. I find that it makes them easier to spot in crowds." He pointed ahead of them to a little nook to one side of the bar, partially hidden by a large sign. Jackson stood side on to them, talking to Kelly.

"And it looks like we've killed two birds with one stone, too," Quinn agreed.

"I was not aware we were looking to hurt birds." Luciano looked at her in confusion, then blinked, clearing his expression, and waving away his bafflement. "Do not worry. Frankie says things like that all the time. I'm guessing you are happy to have found your friend."

Quinn smiled at the likable cowboy. "I am, indeed. Shall we go to them?"

He held his arm out to her. "I think we should."

She couldn't resist admiring Jackson's strong profile, his square jaw looking like it could have been cut from granite. He turned when she and Luciano reached them, and she was amazed she hadn't noticed the cleft in his chin before. She wondered what it felt like to touch, hidden as it was beneath a day's worth of stubble.

"Quinn." His voice was deep and the way he said her name felt strangely intimate. She freed herself of the thought. The man simply said her name, nothing more. "I'm glad you decided to stay for the afterparty after all."

"What? And miss out on my chance to rib you about an Aussie coming out on top? No way!"

A lopsided grin adorned his lips, setting a devilish sparkle to his eyes. "I don't mind the idea of an Aussie being on top at all."

Kelly snorted as Quinn felt her cheeks burn at his mischievous retort. She looked around, noticing a group of girls who were trying to appear innocently nearby rather than stalking their prey—the tall American cowboy.

"I think you won't have any problems with making that happen tonight." Amusement dripped from her voice as she gestured to the nearby buckle bunnies. A funny fluttering of warmth danced in her belly at the flicker of smug interest that flashed across his handsome face before he fully comprehended her words. It was clear he was interested in just the one Aussie—her. As flattering as his attention was, Quinn reminded herself that she had a boyfriend and if he hadn't canceled on her tonight, she would have been out with him, not here with a handsome cowboy. "The announcer said this was the last event of the year for you. What are your plans for what remains of the year?"

Jackson took a sip of his drink. "Head home. I haven't been home for more than a week or two for the last few months."

Quinn wasn't sure if that was a lifestyle she'd particularly enjoy. Sure, it probably started off being exciting, especially when you were young. But after a while it must really wear on a body. "So where exactly is home? I know you're from Colorado?"

"Yeah, my family have a ranch just outside of Colorado Springs." His entire countenance softened when he spoke. It was clear the place and his family were special to him.

"Is it just your mom and dad there?"

His lips quirked. Obviously, there were more. "Well, my

pop and grandma—it was their ranch originally—they still live there. My dad and uncle ran it together, but my uncle died a few years back. My sister and her husband moved back after they got married and they have two kids now."

Quinn could feel her mouth drop open. "That is one crowded house. Christmas morning must be mayhem."

He laughed. This time, his amusement was unable to be contained. "Everyone has their own house, but we all still gather at Mom and Dad's for Christmas Eve and morning. It used to be Pop and Grandma's, but it was getting too much, so Grandma passed the Christmas torch on to Mom. But you're right. It's loud and chaotic and, well"—he shrugged his shoulders as if it explained everything—"it's our family Christmas."

"I think it sounds great. We go back to my parents for Christmas, too, but it's only my brother and his wife and me."

"I spend mine in Bora Bora," Kelly said, joining in the conversation. "So much easier for my mental well-being that way."

"I guess every family have different Christmas traditions," Jackson offered.

"Oh, no, she goes to Bora Bora by herself. I've invited her to mine a few times, but she always insists on going alone."

Luciano looked sadly at her. "I do not like the thought of anyone spending Christmas alone."

Kelly patted the forlorn Brazilian on the arm. "Don't worry about me. I'm rarely alone for long." She gave him a cheeky wink and looked down, feigning surprise to find her glass empty. "I think I need another drink. Can I get anyone else another one?" The others murmured their agreement and Luciano, ever the gentleman, insisted on accompanying her.

Quinn was about to ask Jackson about his ranch when she was abruptly spun around and found herself face to face with a livid Lance. To an outsider, he would have seemed calm, friendly even, but she knew better. There was a flatness to his dark eyes, his lips a little too tight. Quinn felt an uneasy feeling in her stomach. She wasn't sure what had prompted him to leave his little soiree with his clients to come to a rodeo afterparty of all things, but whatever it was didn't bode well for her.

"Come with me," he said, the words tightly clipped together.

Quinn looked over her shoulder at Jackson. There was a tenseness emanating from his tall, strong frame. "Can you please let Kelly know that I'm leaving with Lance?" She smiled, aware that it was too bright, too brittle. "It was a pleasure meeting you." Shoulders bowed, she submissively followed her boyfriend outside until they reached the carpark.

"I will not allow you to disrespect me like you did today," Lance snarled, his face a mask of anger once he was satisfied they were alone. "I had to find out from my friends what you did. It showed up on their social media. How do you think that made me feel, seeing pictures of you draping yourself over strange men? I have to explain your behavior to them. How am I going to do that?"

JACKSON KNEW he should leave it alone. Quinn wasn't his, she was Lance's. But there'd been something dark in her boyfriend's eyes that he hadn't liked. After a brief internal war, he decided his parents hadn't raised him to ignore his gut instinct. Determinedly, he headed out, following the direction he'd seen them take. It wasn't long before he found the pair in the carpark. Foreboding shivered up his spine when he saw Quinn standing, shoulders bowed, in the distance as she faced off against her boyfriend.

As he came closer, she raised her chin defiantly, blinking away tears as she met Lance's eyes. "You can try telling them the truth—that I was doing my job."

Lance's mouth twisted into an ugly sneer. "There's only one job I know of that requires a woman to wear tight, barely-there clothes and rub against strange men." Jackson's blood pounded in his ears, the need to send this weaselly jerk sitting on his backside overpowering.

Quinn gasped at his insinuation. "I was wearing jeans and a top. Don't you dare imply that I was doing anything other than what I was, and that was a promo shoot for a rodeo." Lance was too focused on Quinn, all his anger and loathing targeted at her, that he still hadn't noticed Jackson approaching. Without a word, Lance backhanded Quinn, sending her staggering backwards, her hand flying to her cheek.

Without hesitation, Jackson barreled forward, his fist connecting satisfyingly with the jerk's jaw and sending him sprawling to the ground. Deciding that the man wasn't worth any more of his time, Jackson stood protectively beside Quinn, anger seething through him when he saw the red welt that was already forming on her cheek.

"Are you okay?"

Quinn bit down on her trembling bottom lip, tears welling. She dashed them away, still not looking Jackson in the face. "I'll be fine. He's never done anything like this before."

The anger that snaked through Jackson's belly threatened to bite when he heard her defending the piece of pond scum that she called a boyfriend. "Is this how Australian men treat their women? Because where I come from, he'd get a flogging—one that he richly deserves."

Quinn finally met his gaze, flickers of anger sparking. "Of course not. My dad would never think of hitting my mom."

Jackson's voice softened. "Then why are you letting your boyfriend do this to you?"

"He might act like a jerk sometimes, but he's never done anything like this before. It's just a big misunderstanding." Jackson clenched his jaw, biting down on the fury her quietly spoken words ignited in him.

"You need to go back inside and mind your own business," Lance sneered from behind him.

"It will always be my business when I see a man hit a woman." Jackson hated how Quinn had dropped her eyes again, her face twisting in embarrassment.

"I'm leaving now, Quinn. If you know what's best, you'll come too." Lance held his hand out insultingly and smirked at Jackson as if to say, 'Just watch. I've called, and she'll come,' and then began to walk to his car.

"He isn't always like this," Quinn said again.

"It sounds like you're making excuses for him," Jackson said. He'd only just met Quinn, but the woman who was standing in front of him bore very little resemblance to the sassy woman he'd met that morning.

Quinn smiled sadly at him. "It was nice meeting you. I hope you have a merry Christmas back home at your ranch. It sounds lovely."

She quickly scurried after her boyfriend. Jackson felt like he'd been punched in the gut as he watched her leave with a man who didn't deserve to breathe the same air as her, let alone be her boyfriend. Helplessly, not knowing what else to do, he watched as she climbed into an expensive sportscar and drove off with Lance. Feeling sick to his soul, he grimly headed back inside.

CHAPTER 4

The crackling of the fire could only just be heard over his family's excited chatter as they set up the traditional Christmas Eve board game, their Christmas stockings having been hung with great ceremony on the mantle. Jackson breathed in deeply, inhaling the nutmeg and brandy aroma as he sipped his eggnog, the sweet creamy drink wrapping him in comforting warmth as surely as a soft blanket. He knew that if he opened the curtains, he would find snow gently falling, the snow drifts getting deeper with each hour.

"Does anyone want more eggnog?" Mom called, raising her voice to be heard over the kids' animated discussion of who would be first to roll the dice. "Jimmy, Laura, be careful. I swear, if you spill any cocoa on my rug, I'll send a letter to Santa myself." Mom sternly placed her hands on her hips.

"Mom," Beth, his sister, said. "I think the elves have updated the system and accept emails now."

"Nan, if you send a letter tonight, won't Santa already be in the sleigh delivering presents to other countries? At school, they explained the different time zones. Like, you know how when Uncle Jackson was in Australia and he called home and he was calling from tomorrow? Well that's how it works on Christmas Eve, too."

Mom's eyes bulged, a slight twitch in one of them as she digested his explanation. "Beth, I swear this one is going to be a rocket scientist or something." She smiled fondly at her grandson. "Jimmy, I'm sure you're right. If you spill a single drop of cocoa, I'm gonna call him direct and tell on you." Regally, she spun on her heel and marched back into the kitchen.

"Your mother loves this time of year," Dad said to Jackson. "It gives her more opportunities than usual to be dramatic. It makes her so happy."

"A woman needs a bit of spirit. It's what's made my marriage to your mother so entertaining," Pop said. "A man needs a little spice in his life."

"Ooww, Pop." Laura, the youngest of Beth's kids, covered her ears.

Pop stuck his tongue out. "Well, you shouldn't have been eavesdropping."

"But I'm sitting right here, like, right in front of you. How did you expect me not to hear you?" protested Laura, snatching the dice off her brother to claim her turn.

Jackson had been back home for a couple of weeks now, helping his dad and brother-in-law, Levi, with tasks around the ranch. There had been a lot to do, especially with all the snow that had been forecasted over Christmas. Each day had been spent getting cold, wet and dirty, and yet he never felt happier than when he worked side by side with his family, the dirt of the ranch working its way back into his blood.

The only fly in the ointment had been the persistent thoughts of a beautiful sandy-haired woman. During the day, when his hands were busy with tasks, his mind was free to drift and he would remember her soulful hazel eyes, awash with tears, pleading at him to understand why she was leaving with that jerk she called a boyfriend. At night, it was worse. He worried that she carried other marks of his temper. Mostly, he wanted to know that she was safe and happy.

Jimmy's earlier comment about time set Jackson to doing some swift calculations. That boy was too smart for his own good, but he was right. In Australia, it would already be Christmas day, Santa having completed his present delivery. As he gazed at the twinkling lights on the Christmas tree, the fresh smell of its pine needles washing over him, Jackson pictured Quinn somewhere in Australia, smiling and happy as she exchanged gifts with her loved ones. Yep, he prayed that's what it was like for her and not the alternatives that plagued his mind.

THE PLASTIC of the outdoor furniture refused to release Quinn as she went to rise, her perspiration having glued her skin to its surface. She waved a fly away from her face and headed over to where her dad stood peeling a prawn that he'd retrieved from the pool of slowly melting ice laden with the rest of the seafood.

"Your mom will be out soon with the pavlova and the frozen pudding." He dipped his freshly liberated crustacean into a small bowl of seafood sauce. "You know, there's plenty of food here. If Lance changes his mind, he's more than welcome to come. Heck, he'd help with the numbers for the cricket match later on." Somehow, Quinn didn't think Lance was much of a backyard cricket type of guy. She'd been with him for nearly three years now and slowly felt like he was strangling the joy out of her.

"I don't think he's going to make it, Dad."

Dad chewed, rolling his eyes exaggeratedly, his enjoyment plain. "His loss. What's that now? Three years in a row? Make sure you remember to get his present out from under the tree before you leave. Your mom spent ages trying to get him something just right."

Quinn could only imagine Lance's reaction to the gift that her mother would have put a great deal of thought into selecting for him. She didn't know what it was, but Mom loved Christmas as much as she did and opened her house and festive spirit to everyone equally. Quinn debated whether to take the gift and just not give it to Lance. Maybe tell Mom a fib about how much he loved it. It wasn't like Lance was ever going to see her parents again. He'd made it perfectly clear the one and only time that he'd met them that they weren't his type of people. It probably hadn't helped that her parents were only five years older than him.

Her dad was right. It was his loss. Actually, everything was his loss. Quinn looked around her childhood backyard, decked out in all its Christmas splendor. Through the open sliding doors, she could see the fake Christmas tree, the fiber optic lights still on, a lone present sitting forlornly beneath it. Her brother, Kyle, and his fiancée, Lisa, were using the top of a cricket bat to hammer in the wickets in preparation for the traditional game of backyard cricket the whole family—well, the five of them, she amended—would partake in later.

She smiled as her mother appeared at the door, a pavlova laden with passionfruit and bananas held proudly in front of her. "Quinn, go get the pudding. I've just taken it out of the freezer and I want everyone to have some before it melts. It's gonna be a scorcher soon."

Quinn quickly retrieved it and watched as her loved ones gathered round, complimenting Mom on her desserts, laughing as Dad read a joke from the bon bons they'd opened earlier. Clarity hit her hard. Her family wasn't fancy or flashy, but they were happy and loved each other. Earlier, Lance had tried to rob her of even that, grumbling that she needed to spend the day with him, not here with her family —a family that had invited him to join them as well.

She couldn't keep going on. How she was, here with her family, celebrating Christmas, that was the happy Quinn she wanted to be. Not having to put a brave face on for everyone, saying everything was fine when she felt like she was constantly walking around on eggshells.

Quinn felt fat, sticky drips of sweat roll down her brow. It mixed with the bug spray and sunscreen to produce an odor that was distinctly that of summertime in Australia and laughed as a memory flashed through her mind. Kyle looked at her, his brow quirked, clearly thinking she was over-playing her amusement at their dad's jokes. She waved it off, too happy to bottle it up. The tall Colorado cowboy had been baffled how anyone could feel like it was Christmas when it was this hot. Heck, it had even been cooler, if only a little, on the day they'd done their promo shoot.

Quinn grew somber as she thought back to his last words to her, that it was no way for a woman to be treated. Was she going to allow herself to keep being treated like Lance's doormat, paying the price when she didn't get it right? She squared her shoulders. She was done. A sense of complete contentment filtered through her, like God was blessing her decision, showing her how right it was.

Quinn wondered how Jackson was. She hoped he was happy, spending time back at the ranch that clearly had meant so much to him with his family he loved. It felt strange that it had only been a few weeks ago that she'd met him. For someone who had only for the briefest of moments touched her life, the impact had been profound. He had shown her an example of the type of man she could trust her heart with, one who would treat it like the precious gift it was. He was everything Lance, with his controlling ways and manipulations, wasn't. Calm, humble, and the type of guy who was as dependable as the sun.

She knew that no matter what happened, her life was richer for having met him. It saddened her that it had only been brief, but pragmatically, Quinn decided that sometimes special souls were only meant to pass through, leaving their message in their wake. Maybe he'd been her early Christmas present? Smiling, a warm glow flowed through her. She liked the thought of that, she really did. One thing she did know—it was probably a lot colder where he was.

SEVEN MONTHS LATER, LA ON THE WAY TO LAS VEGAS

"Miss, could you please stow your table? We're about to land."

Quinn started at the flight attendant's words, completely lost in the book she'd been reading. Obediently, she put her table up, yawning as she looked around the cabin. It sure was a bloody long flight from Brisbane to Las Angeles, but the comfort of travel in business class had more than made up for it. She tapped the slumbering Kelly's leg, causing her friend to wake up with a startled snort, hair stuck to the side of her face, very much at odds with her usual polished image. Quinn smothered her laughter. She had so much to be thankful to her friend for.

When she'd broken up with Lance, he'd been smug at first, telling her that she would regret it and come running back in a week. When that hadn't happened and she'd begun luxuriating in the sense of freedom being apart from him had filled her with instead, his anger had smoldered, filling him with sinister intentions. Quinn had only become aware of his intentions when she'd returned to work to find her emails overflowing with requests to work with someone else. It hadn't taken long for her to be called into the manager's office along with Kelly to be told that she'd turned into PR poison and no one was willing to work with her anymore.

Quinn had been furious. Even when they were no longer together, Lance was trying to control her and, ultimately, if he couldn't get her to go back to him, he was going to make her suffer. Kelly had been loyal and insisted that she still needed her, but for the next several long months, Quinn had been stuck at her desk doing the hard slog of paperwork rather than coordinating glamourous events or handling VIP clients.

She still clearly remembered the day Kelly had answered her phone and stood up to go into one of the conference rooms. When she'd returned, she'd grabbed her handbag and told Quinn they were both going out to lunch. Since Kelly had no qualms about putting lunches on her corporate credit card, she hadn't needed to be asked twice. Over a delicious Thai beef salad accompanied by a superb Riesling, the intense acidity of the fruit making her mouth water between sips, Kelly had laid out her plans. And what plans they were.

On the sly, her friend had applied for a position working for The Chimera—one the most high-profile casinos in Las Vegas—to be their PR Manager. Not surprisingly, since Kelly had the Midas touch, she'd been awarded the position and, as part of her negotiations, she'd informed them that she would be bringing her own assistant with her.

"You"—Kelly had pointed her fork at Quinn—"you're coming with me."

Quinn still felt shocked by how matter-of-fact Kelly had been at her earth-shattering, life-changing announcement. Everything after that was a blur. The visa applications, tying up loose ends and then now, finally, sitting on a plane preparing to land.

Nerves began to thrum through Quinn's body as she

stood in line at customs, the excited chatter of tourists flying around her. For a moment, she felt like she couldn't breathe. No matter how bad things had gotten back home, she'd known she could always turn up on Mom and Dad's doorstep, have a cup of tea, maybe a slice of cake, or if she timed it right on a Sunday evening, maybe even a roast lamb dinner. Her family had always been her security blanket. But over here, she was a long way from home. She peeked over at Kelly, fanning herself in the stuffy space with her passport. Well, she wasn't really alone, not by a long shot. Quinn squared her shoulders. *I've got this. I've totally got this.*

~

THEY DIDN'T HAVE THIS. They really didn't.

"I don't know how to get out." Kelly growled in frustration.

"I think you just went past that car again." Quinn's gaze swept the hire car parking lot, desperate to find a way to escape.

"Whose idea was this anyway?"

Quinn stared at Kelly in astonishment. "Um, it was yours. In fact, I tried to argue that it would be better to fly to Vegas, but you were all like, 'How hard could it be? It'll give us a chance to see some of the countryside and'—my personal favorite—'we can bond.' As if I need to bond with you any more." Quinn crossed her arms and stared straight ahead in a huff.

Kelly turned the car sharply, going over a bollard as she lined up the exit point they had been able to see in the distance but, despite their best efforts, had been unable to reach. "You might want to hang on."

The girls' rocky start to getting out of the parking lot was nothing compared to the stomach-churning fear of Kelly driving lost and without a single clue of LA road rules.

"Bloody heck, Kelly, you're on the wrong side of the road," screeched Quinn, almost climbing out of her seat in alarm.

"Do you want to do this?" demanded Kelly, her knuckles white on the steering wheel. "The blooming sat nav isn't moving. I have no idea where I am or how I'm meant to get onto the freeway or even what freeway I'm meant to be on, for that matter." Her voice rose with each mounting issue.

"Okay, you need to pull over, and we both need to calm down."

Kelly's eyes were slightly wild when she finally managed to bring the car to a stop. "No, what I need to do is return this bloody car and head back to the airport. We're flying to Vegas."

Quinn pressed her lips together, slightly in shock at her friend's harried state. There was no way she was willing to drive. It had, after all, been Kelly's idea to do this road trip. But now that they'd committed to doing it, she felt honor-bound to help make it happen. "Take a few deep breaths. I'm going to see if I can get this sat nav to work." Quinn did the only thing she knew how—she turned it off, counted to ten and turned it back on again. Thankfully, it rebooted and showed them at a different location to where it had frozen before. "See? It's working."

Kelly appeared to be doing some intense soul searching on her side of the vehicle. "I don't know if I can do this."

"Of course you can. Now, let's get to Las Vegas." Quinn clapped her hands together, channeling her best inner cheerleader.

Kelly nodded determinedly and put the windscreen wipers on. With a muttered curse, she turned them off and managed to get the indicator on. Quinn settled back in her seat, the armpits of her shirt uncomfortably damp from her nerves. It was going to be a long day.

THE TRUCKS and cars merging and flying off on ramps at great speed meant that Quinn was constantly on the edge of her seat, trying to make sure she saw anything that Kelly might miss. She felt like she was in a constant state of anxiety. If she'd hoped that they would hit the open road fast, she was sadly mistaken. The sprawling metropolis of the City of Angels seemed reluctant to let them escape from its clutches.

At last they were free, and Quinn was surprised to find the road going up as they headed through a mountain pass, the countryside around them dry. Once they reached the top, the land flattened out. More mountains could be seen in the distance, but it was otherwise barren. From time to time, they would see run-down houses along the side of the road and the odd truck stop, but nothing more.

"I can't believe how everyone seems to have a big Tonka truck," Kelly noted, having finally calmed down enough to accept a piece of candy from Quinn. "It makes me feel itty bitty in this little hire car."

"Yeah, and all the big fifth wheelers on the road. They're all bloody huge." Quinn's tummy began to rumble, reminding her that she'd only eaten candy since they'd landed and only airline food for the fifteen hours before that.

"It looks like there might be a place to stop up ahead," Kelly said, pointing to a sign in the distance. "I think we could both do with something to eat."

There was no way Quinn was going to argue with that. As they pulled into the parking lot of the lonesome diner, she peered up at the sign. *Peggy Sue's*. Judging from all the cars already pulled up even though it was in the middle of nowhere, it must have something going for it.

Pins and needles shot up her leg as she put weight on it. Quinn gasped, staggering to rebalance herself.

Kelly snorted. "You all right there?"

"Fine, thanks for the sympathy. Are we going to head in or what?"

"After you, hoppy," Kelly said with an enormous grin. Quinn shook her head, pretending to be disappointed at her friend's enjoyment of the situation.

As they pushed through the doors, Quinn could feel herself gawking. Loud fifties music was playing, the décor set in the same decade. One side was a little gift and candy shop and the other was the diner. "Are you going to stand here like a stunned mullet, or are you going in?" grumbled Kelly, pushing past her and walking up to the counter.

A waitress who looked like she'd stepped straight from a *Happy Day's* episode handed them a menu as she passed, coffee pot in hand, ready to fill up a customer's cup further down. Quinn's eyes went wide when she noticed the row of pies in the cabinet on the back wall. "Oh, my."

"Hi, honey, what can I get you today?" The waitress returned having seen to the other customer's needs.

"Well, this is the first time I've ever been to America and definitely the first time I've ever been to a place like this," Quinn said as she took a seat. "What would you recommend?"

The waitress tapped her pencil on the laminate counter. "Well, Peggy Sue's is known for its pies." Quinn found the woman's slow drawl charming. There was a cadence to it that was like slow molasses on a cold day.

"Like a meat pie?" Kelly asked. "We know all about them from back home."

The waitress gave a tinkle of laughter. "No, honey." The

woman's long inhale should have warned them of the list that was to follow. "We have key lime pie, blueberry custard pie, chocolate cream pie, apple pie, lemon meringue pie, vinegar pie, strawberry rhubarb pie"—another dramatic pause for more breath as she continued to tick them off her fingers—"chocolate walnut pie, pecan pie, banana cream pie and cherry pie."

Quinn knew her eyes must be glazed over after the pie menu had been recited to her. She had no earthly idea where to begin. "Um, Kelly, what are you going to have?"

"I think I'm going to have to try a slice of your cherry pie." Kelly nodded her head decisively before raising a questioning brow in her direction. "What about you?"

"I'd like to try the chocolate cream pie, please." Chocolate being Quinn's go-to favorite dessert flavor meant it was a pretty safe choice.

"And what can I grab you to drink?" The waitress took their menus off them, her pencil held to her pad in anticipation of their answer.

"Do you have tea?" Quinn asked.

"Sure do."

"We'll both have one," Kelly said, answering for them both.

"Sure thing, honey. I'll bring you both a glass of sweet tea."

Quinn looked at Kelly, confused at the concept of tea coming in a glass. "She didn't even ask if we wanted sugar, how does she know we'll want it sweet?"

"Maybe she thought you needed sweetening up?"

"She's bringing you one, too," Quinn retorted.

"But I'm sweet enough, honey." Kelly did a decent impression of the waitress's voice, sending Quinn into a coughing fit of laughter. It was nice to feel … free? Like she didn't have to look over her shoulder all the time.

"We did it," Kelly said, accepting her drink from the waitress and staring down at it in confusion. "Um, it's cold."

The waitress looked at her like she was simple. "It's sweet tea."

"Oh, that makes sense, I guess." Dubiously, Kelly took a sip. "It is, indeed, very sweet tea." Satisfied, the waitress took some pies out of the display cabinet and began to cut a slice from each.

"It's nice to not be worried about what Lance will do next," Quinn said, taking a sip of her own drink. The saccharine sweetness stuck to her tongue.

"At least I know you're safe with an ocean between you and that loser." Quinn couldn't have said it better. Kelly gripped her hand. "We're going to have the time of our lives here, Quinn. It's going to be awesome."

Later, as the glittering Strip came into view, right on sunset with mountains providing a spectacular backdrop, Kelly's words came back to Quinn. She certainly hoped her friend was right. She could do with a little awesome in her life right now.

CHAPTER 6

The valet in his red coat with gold trim took their keys with a quick nod of his head before he was on his way. Quinn stuck close to Kelly as they walked into the lobby of The Chimera Casino. She felt nervous about making a good impression with both her employer and her fellow employees. She'd been shocked when Kelly had informed her that, as part of their contract, she'd negotiated for them to share a two-bedroom apartment in the actual casino. Kelly had worded it in such a way that Quinn wasn't sure if it was going to be a good thing or a bad thing. Her exact phrasing had been, "I told them that we would be available and on call twenty-four hours a day and, with the high rollers and performers, I know that will be something the management will appreciate."

Kelly strode up to the concierge desk, all polite business, and introduced herself. The lady behind the desk smiled warmly, calling her boss to let them know the new PR manager had arrived. After she hung up the phone, she looked curiously up at the two travel-weary women.

"I'm Julie, the head concierge here. I'm sure we'll get to

know each other a lot better over the next little while. If you need anything, you let me know."

"Thank you, Julie, that's very kind of you. Quinn here is my assistant and will also be host to the high rollers. I'm sure she'll be very grateful for any assistance you're able to give her as she finds her feet," Kelly said smoothly.

"Hi, Julie. Once we get settled in, it would be great if we could catch up and you can explain to me how things work here. I'm pretty sure it's unlike anywhere else I've ever worked." Quinn looked around. There was a constant stream of people from all walks of life parading through the foyer. It was definitely not going to be boring.

"Kelly, Quinn." A small, immaculately dressed man emerged from a side door, his manicured hand extended. "I'm Lachlan Fitzgerald. We spoke several times on the phone," he reminded Kelly as if she'd somehow managed to forget the name of her new boss. "I hope your flight wasn't too arduous."

"It wasn't the flight that was arduous, more like the driving that made me fear for my life," Quinn muttered under her breath. When he looked quizzically at her, she smiled disarmingly back.

"You'll have to excuse Quinn. She quite often thinks she's funny when she's not." Kelly sent her a stern look.

"Oh, a comedian," Lachlan said with aplomb. "Well, Vegas is the place to be if you're one. That, and a showgirl." Quinn choked a little at the last comment. "Now, I imagine after your journey to get here, you will be quite fatigued. Your accommodation has been prepared for you. If you ladies are ready, I'll take you up now."

A short elevator ride took them to their destination. "This is one of the premier suites, but I feel that, given its proximity to the high roller penthouses, it would be the most suited for your purposes."

Quinn nodded, struck mute by the room she found herself in, barely registering what Kelly replied to Lachlan before he left them to get settled in. Large glass floor-to-ceiling windows looked down on the famed Las Vegas Strip. A mass of humanity flowed down the sidewalks on each side as unstoppable as a river. At one end, Quinn could make out volcanos of fire spewing up into the night sky. Further down, beautifully synchronized jets of water danced. She wistfully imagined the music the fountains frolicked to.

"I don't think we're in Kansas anymore."

Kelly came and stood beside her, staring at the vista below. "We never were. We've just done the easy part—getting here. The hard work starts in a few days. But till then, I say we order some room service, and while we wait, there's a hot shower with my name on it. I think I maybe have another hour left in me before I crash. Tomorrow we can get the lay of the land here in The Chimera and go check out The Strip."

Quinn couldn't have agreed with her friend more. No longer able to resist the siren call of the hot shower to her exhausted body, she nodded. Casting one last glance down at the bright lights that held her future, she wondered what, exactly, that might be.

THE NEXT FEW days went by in a whirlwind of insanely bright lights. The girls' apartment could have been taken straight from the advertising brochure for the high-end suites of the casino. Everything was sleek, glossy and opulent. Every morning, Quinn poured herself a cup of tea and stood sipping it, looking out at the scene below. In the evenings, she enjoyed watching the sun set over the mountains that stood sentry like over the never-ending light show of The Strip.

Amongst all the tackiness that was The Las Vegas Strip—and there was plenty—Quinn found moments where it felt like she'd been dropped into another planet. There was an aroma that, after spending ten minutes following in someone's smoke cloud, always gave her the munchies. She'd been ecstatic to discover a food van parked up beside one of the competitor casinos that sold nothing but different flavored cookie doughs. Later, after walking through the maze of gaming rooms in another casino that had been an original from back in the mafia days, she'd been amazed to discover flamingos and hummingbirds set amongst manmade ponds. Las Vegas was crazy!

And so was the shopping! A town that had been built on gambling knew how to get the last dime out of anyone who had managed to break lucky. Quinn spent an enjoyable afternoon trawling through the high-end fashion shops, drooling over clothes, handbags and shoes while expressionless, tall, skinny attendants watched on. She and Kelly may have spent a little more than was wise, given they'd only just relocated and should have been keeping a bit of a nest egg just in case. Kelly had soothed any concerns with a very airy declaration of, "We need to look the part. Consider it an investment." After her friend's encouraging and sage words, Quinn found it considerably easier to hand her credit card over.

But all good things must come to an end, and this was the first day that reality had hit Quinn. Today, she started work. Pressing her lips one final time to blot her lipstick, she gave a quick check to make sure the nude rose color hadn't migrated to her teeth.

"Are you ready, Kelly?" she called as she slipped her black patent pumps on her feet, admiring the way the red sole contrasted against the sleek inkiness of the leather.

"As ready as I'll ever be," Kelly said, stepping from her room at the same time as Quinn did, meeting each other in the hall. "How do I look?" She gave a slow twirl.

"Like a million bucks." It was true, Kelly had always had a knack for being stylish. Heck, she could make Target look haute couture, but now, compliments of their getting-to-know-Vegas shopping trip, she'd stepped it up to the next level.

"Well, considering how much this outfit cost, I hope so." Kelly paused, her gaze sweeping over Quinn as she gave her the once-over, nodding in satisfaction. "You look great. Those high rollers aren't going to know what hit them."

"That's the plan." Quinn's hand crept to her hair to reassure herself that not a strand was out of place in her sleek bun.

"Well, I'd say you nailed it. Let's get going then."

Quinn tried to keep her nerves under control as they rode the elevator down to the control room of the casino. She desperately hoped she wouldn't perspire all over her new clothes. After all, they wanted to give the illusion that they were perfectly in control, even if it didn't necessarily reflect the truth of the internal emotions.

The doors opened with a ping, and Quinn followed Kelly curiously into the control room. A wall was taken up with giant screens, each one flickering between different viewpoints of the various locations. Some had smudges of reds and oranges over them—heatmaps, she assumed. Lachlan rose from where he'd been seated beside a large man and approached.

"Good morning, ladies. I hope you're as eager to begin as I am."

"Can't wait to get our hands dirty," Kelly said.

"I thought it would be best to start the day here in the brain of the operations. It will give a good overview of things. And then, Kelly, you'll come with me, and Quinn, I'll get you to spend some time with Julie."

"That sounds good," Quinn agreed.

"First, let me introduce you to Nate O'Brien. He's the head of security here. Quinn in particular, if you need help with any of the high rollers who might be getting a bit big for their shoes, call him directly to deal with it."

Quinn looked at the large man who turned at his introduction. Nate had the look of someone who had seen combat, an assurance that he was capable of handling whatever came his way and it might be best not to ask too many questions with how he'd dealt with it when the dust settled. His brown hair was closely clipped to his scalp, light flecks of silver on the side. Quinn put his age somewhere between thirty-five and fifty. His brown eyes were direct and steady, and Quinn liked him immediately.

"It will be my pleasure to assist in any way I can," he said in gravelly tones.

"Now, as I was saying, this is the brains of The Chimera. There isn't a thing that happens in this building that we don't know about up here," Lachlan continued.

"Except what you get up to in the bathroom and, even then, we could find out if we really needed to," Nate added. Quinn wasn't sure if that necessarily reassured her or not.

Lachlan gave a sweeping gesture taking in the screens on the walls. "We have, up here, the gaming rooms, including the high stakes room." He gave a little nod in Quinn's direction. "Shops, restaurants, reception areas, entrances and carparks."

"I can also see the VIP access and the ones security use," Nate said. "Tomorrow, I'll take you ladies to see them and give you swipe card access for them. Quinn, some of your high rollers will expect to only move through the casino via that network."

Quinn nodded, her mind agog at the concept of secret corridors and passages. "Does it come with a treasure map and skeleton key as well?"

"You might find the odd body down there, but no treasure," Nate deadpanned.

"Nate, if you want to give Kelly and Quinn their temporary swipe cards and take their photos and prints for the files, I think we can let Quinn head on downstairs to Julie."

Quinn was a little taken aback at the idea of having her fingerprints on record, but the process was over quickly, and then she found herself once again in the elevator and on her way to the concierge.

The staccato click-clack of Quinn's heels announced her arrival, making Julie look up with a smile. "I love your shoes."

"Thanks, I only got them yesterday. My feet aren't thanking me right now for choosing them for my first day, but they were just too gorgeous not to wear."

"How have you settled in?" Julie stood, grabbing some keys from a drawer.

"It still feels like we're here on a holiday. I don't think reality has hit yet."

"Well it will soon, believe me. Now, I think we'll start in the high roller suite and work our way down. If I forget anything, just stop me and ask."

Quinn fell into step beside Julie as she led the way back to the elevator. A quick ride and then Julie opened the door and, try as she might to appear like this was a world she was used to inhabiting, her jaw dropped open at the sight.

"I know, girl. I did the same thing when I saw it for the first time. Seriously though, some of the people who stay here treat it like trash. It makes me so mad."

Everything about the room screamed opulence and money. A single step into the room had Quinn's feet sinking into the plush carpet. She couldn't be sure, but she suspected that some sort of very expensive perfume had been used as air freshener. She took in the state-of-the-art entertainment system, the artistic gas fireplace, artwork that was so abstract she just knew it had to be expensive. A kaleidoscope of tropical fish swam in an aquarium larger than most people's bed. Wide eyes took in the floor-to-ceiling windows, much like the one in her own room, the extra height affording the lucky occupant even more access to the vista below. The room looked like it easily had enough seating for twenty people.

Quinn closed her mouth, swallowing the dryness away. "Well, it shouldn't be too hard to keep my clients happy in a room like this."

Julie laughed, beckoning her to follow. "You have a lot to learn. Let's just say that it doesn't matter what we offer, the people we deal with, they feel like being difficult is how we poor folk know that they're special. Now, this suite has four double bedrooms and the master." With that, she grandly swung open the double doors of the aforementioned master bedroom.

The bed was easily the largest Quinn had ever seen, the linen screaming a high thread count and silky softness. Another entertainment system, yet another gas fireplace, sweeping views, and the ensuite bathroom that was bigger than Quinn's first apartment. But the pièce de résistance was the private terrace off the master, complete with a private plunge pool.

"Now, when there are guests in this suite, they are your responsibility. You will be who they call for EVERYTHING." Julie rolled her eyes dramatically for extra emphasis. "That room you were given, well, after a while you're going to hate being this close and always at some client or another's beck and call."

Quinn felt herself frown at the other woman's foreboding

pronouncement. "I believe they will have access to room service and yourself as well."

"Yeah, they do. There's also a butler called Dave, and some of them are pretty good. They call for their own food, aren't a bother to anyone. Actually, most of the whales are like that. If you didn't know what their bankroll was, you'd have no idea how wealthy they are. Others want to be a bother. Usually, the single men are the worst, and a pretty thing like you are going to have your hands full. They will be calling you, not Dave." Julie pointed at Quinn. "They will want you to look after them like rich, spoiled babies." Seemingly satisfied that she'd made her point, she headed toward the door. "Now, let's go and meet some of the people you are going to get to know very well while looking after these babies."

The rest of the tour flashed by in a blur of rooms, a labyrinth of the behind-the-scenes corridors, private areas, elevators and high stakes gambling rooms. Names and faces tumbled together as Quinn lay in bed that night, her feet throbbing and blistered. Marie, Dave, Bobby, Ian—or was it Eddie? She had never been so grateful that most of the staff wore name badges. Mentally drained, she fell into an exhausted slumber, haunted by the smiling blue eyes of a cowboy she'd never forgotten.

CHAPTER 7

"Marie, I know we haven't known each other that long, but I think I love you," Quinn declared, closing her eyes as she savored the last creamy morsel of the crème brûlée éclair. The filling was silkily smooth against the richness of the burnt caramel.

Marie, the head pastry chef, smiled at her, a light dusting of confectionary sugar on her nose. "You'd be surprised how often I get that, and before you ask, I don't think we'd last." She came closer and stared deeply into Quinn's eyes. "All we have is the sugar."

Quinn burst out laughing, Marie giving her a saucy wink as she returned to measuring out her ingredients. "I think I need to start visiting the gym more. It's that or stop visiting the kitchen for your creations, and we both know that won't happen."

The slap of the kitchen doors being pushed upon caused Quinn to guiltily lick her fingers to remove all traces of evidence. Eddie, the pit boss, strolled in, a two-way radio in hand. "Somehow, I thought I might find you in here," he greeted Quinn.

"Just making sure that everything is shipshape for when I have my first guest to look after," Quinn said, subtly rubbing her ever-so-slightly sticky fingers together. Deciding the ruse was up, she popped a macaroon into her mouth, the explosion of strawberry mint so delicious she had to fight the temptation to close her eyes in ecstasy. "Keep up the good work, Marie."

Marie giggled as she started adding her ingredients—or as Quinn liked to think of it, her magical ingredients—into the large mixer. "I'll try."

"Quinn, we've just had word that Markus Jamison will be here in under an hour. You need to check in with Julie to see if he has sent in any requests ahead. She'll also give you a rundown on what his usual tastes are." He smirked at her, clearly knowing something she didn't. "Good luck, kid."

"Um, okay," Quinn mumbled, heading for the door. "I guess I'll go find Julie."

As usual, the head concierge was ensconced behind her desk. "Quinn, I'm glad to see you. Did Eddie send you?"

"Yeah, he mentioned something about a high roller coming in?" Quinn perched herself on the cold counter. "What do I need to know?"

"The high roller isn't just any high roller. He's a whale, and his name is Markus Jamison."

Quinn still wasn't all over the casino lingo yet. *A whale? Was the high roller overly large? Had a huge appetite?* "What's a whale?"

"A whale is someone who has a gambling bankroll of over one million dollars. Markus's is substantially more than that." Julie's smile seemed slightly strained, as though she wasn't sure about something. Worried, perhaps.

"Okay, Julie, spill. There's a lot more you need to tell me." Quinn folded her arms across her chest.

"Markus can be … well, he's one of our most demanding

guests." Julie's nose wrinkled as she spoke, giving Quinn the impression that she was searching for the right words. "Nothing is ever good enough for him, and he demands the utmost attention."

"I'll give him so much attention, he won't know what to do with it." Quinn picked up a notepad from the desk. "Now, tell me everything you know about him."

THE SLEEK, black limo pulled alongside the curb. Quinn could see herself and Randy, the valet, reflected back at them in the dark tint of the car's window. The valet walked forward and opened the door. A moment later, the whale, Markus Jamison, emerged. Quinn's first impression was the man had style and money. In her short time in Vegas, she'd learned that the two were not mutually exclusive. Dark shades hid his eyes as he stood, buttoning up his jacket, surveying his domain. Quinn felt rather than saw the moment his gaze locked on her. Suddenly nervous, she felt her mouth go dry as she strode forward.

"Hi, I'm Quinn Williamson. I'll be your host for your stay."

He stared at her a moment longer, making her feel decidedly off balance before slowly removing his sunglasses, his gaze on her the entire time. Quinn felt like it was the slowest reveal she'd ever been on the receiving end of. Light brown eyes swept her from head to foot and back up again. Feeling herself grow angry at his rudeness, she raised an eyebrow haughtily at him.

"Like what you see?"

"It's a definite improvement on what I had last time."

Quinn plastered a stiff smile on her face, trying not to rise to the bait. She was a professional, after all. "If you would like to come with me, Randy will get your luggage and follow us up to your room."

"I don't think Randy needs to rush. I don't want him interrupting us." A challenge smoldered out at her.

Quinn felt her spine stiffen. He had some nerve. "I really don't think there's going to be anything for him to interrupt. Now, if you'd care to come with me, Eddie will also be meeting us at your suite to sign over your credit." With a sharp pivot on her high heels, she set off toward the VIP elevator, beginning to suspect it was going to be a long couple of days with this jerk of a whale to babysit.

It surprised her that he was beside her in only a few strides. A few after that, he was slightly in front. Not enough to have overtaken her, but just enough to convey that he was in control, not her. When they reached the elevator, he graciously gestured for her to press the button. Quinn knew the look she cast him was severely unamused and not professional, but she couldn't help herself.

He laughed, obviously enjoying her discomfort. "You haven't been in Las Vegas long, have you?"

"No," she managed to grind out. *Where the bloody heck is this elevator?*

"You can tell. You don't have the dead mask everyone gets after they've been here for a while. You'd be no good at cards." The ping announcing the arrival of the lift saved Quinn from having to make a reply as she swiped her access card and pressed the button. Markus stood a fraction too close—not enough that Quinn felt she could protest, but enough to make her feel uncomfortable.

It was with great relief that, upon their arrival, she saw Eddie waiting for them. "I'll leave you in Eddie's capable hands. The high stakes room has been informed of your arrival. The bar fridge has been stocked with Cristal and a bottle of your favorite Tequila Ley has also been placed in the bar for your pleasure. Now, I'll let you get settled in before you hit the tables." She smiled at Eddie and turned for the elevator and freedom from this pompous jerk.

"I wouldn't go too far if I were you, Quinn Williamson." Her brisk steps stopped at his words, dread settling into her stomach at what he might say next. "I think I'm going to need your assistance a great deal while I'm here." Quickly, Quinn stepped into the elevator before he could say more.

THE HIGH ROLLER suite number flashed on Quinn's phone, making her groan. It had only been an hour since she'd left, and she'd already checked with Eddie that Markus had made his way to the high stakes room. Sighing deeply, she answered it. "Hello, Markus. What can I help you with?"

"I'm thirsty."

Quinn felt her eye start to twitch. "I'll let one of the room stewards know and they can arrange a drink for you. Any preferences?"

"I want you to make it for me."

"I'm not really good at mixing drinks."

"Are you any good at drinking?"

Quinn wasn't sure how to get out of the loop she was stuck in. Why didn't the man want to gamble? "I've been known to have a drink or two," she responded evenly.

"Then tell that lady at the front desk to arrange the experience. The one they organized for me last time. Tell her I want it for two, and you, well, I want you dressed and ready to go."

The tone of his voice set her teeth on edge. "Dressed ready for what?"

"Ready for me to enjoy."

That was too much! "Mr Jamison, that's not part of my job."

"Relax, I just want you to come out and have some drinks with me, enjoy yourself. Who knows, you might even loosen up a bit. I want you ready to leave in an hour." The line went dead.

Quinn made her way to Julie's station in record time. "Markus has requested the same experience he had last time. Apparently, it revolved around drinking and he rather enjoyed it."

Julie tapped away at her keyboard, opening screens for reservations. "Oh, the VIP cocktails. When does he want it organized for?"

"He wants it to begin in an hour, and the booking is to be made for two." Quinn felt her mouth pucker like she'd been sucking on lemons.

Julie took one glance at her face and grimaced. "How are you managing with him?"

"Well, I'm the plus one for his little drinking experience this evening."

"Quinn, can I please see you for a moment?" Lachlan called from a side door. Quinn sighed, and Julie stared at her in concerned sympathy.

"Yes, sir."

He closed the door behind her as she stepped through. "This won't take very long. I've just had a call from Markus Jamison. He reminded me that there were plenty of other casinos he could be spending his money in and that he didn't feel like he was getting the attention from his host that he would expect."

"But Lachlan, he wants—" Her boss held up his hand for silence, cutting her off mid-explanation.

"I don't care what he wants. What I care about is how much money he gambles when he stays here. As long as it isn't illegal or completely immoral, which can be a bit of a gray area. I expect you to arrange, organize, or do whatever he requests. Do I make myself clear?"

"Yes, Lachlan." Quinn stared at her boss's chest, afraid that if she made eye contact with him, he'd seen the fury glaring out. As it was, she could feel her lips press into a thin flat line.

"Good. Quinn, I think you can go far with us here, but you need to play by the rules."

"The rules that say the whale is always right," Quinn said sullenly.

"The rules that say the whale is always right," Lachlan agreed. "Now, I believe you need to get ready to accompany Markus for drinks."

~

"I SEE you've managed to find something appropriate to wear after all."

If looks could kill, Markus would have been a dead man. Instead, he stood, checking his cuff links and wearing one of his expensive suits.

"Our limo is waiting, if you're ready." Quinn decided that her best tactic was not to let him see how much he got to her and get through the evening as quickly as possible. "A private table has been booked at the Flynn Club."

"Well, stop frowning, I wouldn't want you to get wrinkles on that pretty face of yours. Who knows?" Markus leaned in close, wrapping a strand of hair around his finger. "You might even enjoy yourself."

Quinn jerked her hair out of his grasp. "Anything's possible with enough bloody alcohol."

The Flynn had a frenetic energy that only a Las Vegas club could muster, from the strobe lights to the scantily clad women pulsing to the beat as the DJ spun his tracks. Quinn had to admit it was cool, despite herself, as the club hostess guided them to their booth. In fact, if she were here with Kelly or anyone else on the entire planet except for the arrogant jerk she was being forced to accompany, she would be getting excited for an amazing night. Quinn glared at the man who was seating himself beside her. Anyone, even her grandma. Well, that wasn't fair. Grandma Beth rocked. But *anyone* except him.

"What drinks can I get you?" The buxom hostess leaned in, her considerable assets in danger of spilling free.

"The lovely lady and I are interested in a ménage à trois." Quinn almost exploded with rage, starting to stand. That was a line she would not cross, no matter the pressure Lachlan was putting on her to keep the client happy. Markus looked amused at her hostility, only fueling it further. "Sit down, sweetheart, before you embarrass yourself. It's just a drink." His voice dripped condensation at her ignorance.

"Oh." She sat down with a little thud.

"Oh, honey." The hostess's eyes went wide in protest, her fake nails moving to rest against her chest. "It's not just any drink. It's the most expensive one we offer. It comes with liquid gold and 23-carat gold flakes scattered on top. The straw has a diamond encrusted logo on it that you get to take home."

"Sounds expensive." Quinn wondered if her expense account covered drinks.

"Oh, it is. Each drink costs three thousand dollars."

Quinn's jaw dropped a little. Markus's smug look of enjoyment was enough to make it snap shut. "I'm not sure that Lachlan has given me enough funds to cover that drink."

"And that's why everything is on me tonight. You should count yourself lucky. Usually, I expect everything to be comped." Markus looked like he expected her to heap gratitude at his feet. Well, he was going to wait a bloody long time if he thought she was going to do that.

Markus waved the hostess away and looked over at the dance floor. "Usually I'm out there, surrounded by beautiful women."

Quinn looked at him in disgust. "I'm not stopping you. In fact, I insist you go."

He smirked back at her. "I'm having too much fun watching you endure my company."

The hostess brought the drinks back and Quinn had to give it to them—it looked like liquid sunshine that had been captured in a glass. Cautiously, she took a sip through her diamond accented straw, the intoxicating nectar sliding smoothly down her throat, a delicious warmth following. She looked up to find Markus watching her intently. "Well, did you enjoy your first ménage à trois ?"

"I think it is a very expensive drink, but it's amazing," Quinn was forced to admit.

"I knew you would, you naughty little minx. Now, finish it up and don't forget to grab your straw. We have more obscenely expensive cocktails to introduce you to."

And what followed was a whirlwind of drinks in small glasses and tall glasses, glasses aflame, and floating in saucers of dry ice. Each exponentially more elaborate than the last. And then, when Quinn thought she'd seen it all and was, admittedly, held fast in a warm, fuzzy glow, they approached their final destination, The Bravo Lounge, where the evening reached its pinnacle.

"This one"—Markus made a kissing motion against his fingers—"it will blow your mind."

"Markus, I've lost track of all the mind-blowing drinks I've had tonight." Quinn was beginning to feel a little bleary eyed.

"It's called the Yoko and it is the most expensive cocktail you can buy in Vegas."

"Well, it's about time we finished with drinking all that cheap and nasty stuff." Quinn waited while the hostess took their order. "Does the hangover feel the same when the cocktails cost this much?"

"About ten times worse," Markus admitted. "The secret is to just not stop drinking."

Quinn laughed. "I couldn't afford to keep drinking like this."

"Stick with me and you won't have to worry about affording anything." His gaze drifted to the far end of the room, a crease forming on his brow.

"Markus, no amount of money is going to make you less of a jerk or make me want to stick anywhere near you."

"Ouch." He held his hand to his chest in mock wounding, his pinky ring catching the light. "If I had a heart, that would've hurt."

Quinn's head snapped around at the sudden commotion of sparklers and bells. A procession of what looked to be over twenty people were headed their way. A manager held a wooden box carefully in front of him while the original hostess held a bottle of champagne and another held a tray with glassware. Stunned, Quinn turned back to Markus.

"Are they coming for us?"

"Wait and see." He smirked at her.

The tray was set down in front of them. It contained gold-rimmed champagne flutes and several shot glasses that held a variety of different liquids in them. With great ceremony, the manager opened the box to reveal a black bottle and carefully poured out a measure in two of the shot glasses that had remained empty. Next, he poured the contents of all of them into the champagne flutes. The hostess opened the champagne bottle with a saber, the cork shooting off like a rocket as a river of foaming liquid cascaded out. Once it was under control, the flutes were topped up. Two velvet boxes were handed over gravely, and then the entire procession wordlessly bowed and departed.

Quinn wasn't entirely sure what had just happened. It had been the most surreal cocktail presentation she'd ever seen. Incredulous, she looked at Markus. "How much, exactly, does this thing cost?" She pointed urgently at the drink in front of her.

"Ten thousand dollars. But we do get to keep the bottle of cognac and, for the lady"—he opened the velvet box in front of her to reveal a gleaming necklace with a single black pearl pendant—"and for the gentleman." He opened his to show a pair of stingray leather cufflinks. "So, you could say this one is good value for money. Now, have a drink."

It was beautiful, the glassware delicate in her hand as she sipped it. A gorgeous pairing of champagne and cognac fizzed in her mouth deliciously. "It's indescribable."

"Just like spending the evening with me. I knew you wouldn't be able to resist me for too long." Markus's tone was insulting, like he was under the delusion that, somewhere over the course of the evening, he'd acquired her.

Quinn almost spat her crazy-expensive drink all over him. She stared at him like he'd just grown another head. "The only reason I'm here is because Lachlan told me I wouldn't have a job at the casino if I didn't, and he only told me that after you talked to him. Let me guess, this little show of extravagance, the flashing of your money, huge tips along the way, it normally gets the girls all over you. Or if that doesn't work, what? You just force girls to go on dates with you. That's pathetic. And guess what? I don't like it. The money, all of this"—Quinn did a sweeping gesture with her hands—"doesn't make me like you any more. See, I know your type. Heck, my last boyfriend was exactly your type. So, let me put it to you in a way you will understand. I'm not buying what you're selling. Now, if you'll excuse me, I'm done here." Majestically, she stood, regal in her outrage, grabbed her champagne flute and emptied what remained of its ten-thousand-dollar contents in a single gulp. "Good night." Without another look at Markus, she snatched her necklace from the table and waltzed from the room.

Quinn could only pray that he'd spend the next day gambling. To a certain extent, she'd got her wish, but it hadn't stopped him making several demands that set her teeth on edge. He'd informed the stewardess that he would accept his drinks from Quinn, and so she'd spent the better part of the day standing to one side of the room, waiting for his beckoning gesture that he required another beverage. By the fourth hour of his boorish behavior, she began to fantasize about dumping the contents of his next order over his obnoxious head. Her intent must have shown on her face as Eddie sent her a threatening glare.

Quinn sighed as she approached the table. Markus's arm snaked around her waist and pulled her in close, sending ripples of distaste through her body. "What can I say? I think I've found my lucky charm." He raked in his winnings, neatly stacking them into piles. "Now, you gentlemen will have to excuse me. I have lunch plans with a beautiful lady." He slapped her on the bum.

She could feel her nostrils flare at the attack on her rigid person. That was it. He'd taken it too far, and she was going to give him what for.

Eddie beckoned her. "If I might have a moment of Quinn's time before you abscond with her." Graciously, like some sort of benevolent overlord, Markus gestured his approval.

Quinn forced herself to relax her clenched jaw. She didn't want to chip a tooth on this jerk's behalf. "Thanks for rescuing me, Eddie. No way was I going to bloody lunch with him."

The sweet sense of relief to be freed from his churlish clutches was short-lived. "I think you misunderstand, Ms Williamson. I wanted to remind you that Mr Jamison is a very valuable guest to The Chimera Casino and I expect you to do everything in your power to keep him happy and give him a reason to continue bringing his bankroll to this establishment. Do I make myself clear?"

Quinn was the first to break eye contact. "Yes."

"Good. Now run along, I don't want you keeping him waiting."

As she made her way alongside Markus, he reached his hand around. Quinn wasn't sure if his intent was to grab her or slap her on the bum again. Either way, she wasn't taking any chances. "If you touch me again, I'll bloody break your fingers so you can't play poker ever again"—she held up a restraining finger—"and before you mention my job, it would be worth it and the likely jail time that would follow."

Markus laughed, setting her teeth on edge. "I like them feisty. It's more of a challenge. Now, I hope you like burgers."

She would rather die than admit that burgers were one of her favorite things in the world. "I eat them from time to time."

"Then I think you'll like this." Taking his life into his own hands, he took her elbow and guided her out into the crowded Las Vegas Strip.

A short walk led them to a competitor casino, past expensive shops that, any other time, Quinn would have loved to window shop at, knowing her wage didn't extend to any purchases, and into an incredibly upmarket restaurant. She was confused why Markus had asked her if she liked burgers and then brought her to a place like this.

"Ah, Markus, my good friend. I am pleased to see you again." The world-renowned head chef greeted Markus like he was an old friend. It made Quinn want to be sick.

"Henri, I wouldn't come to Vegas and not see you."

Henri turned knowing eyes to Quinn. "I see you have brought a beautiful friend for company. Mademoiselle"—he bowed over her hand—"it will be my honor to serve you today." Despite herself, Quinn couldn't help smiling at the charming Frenchman. After pressing a kiss to her hand, Henri returned his attention to Markus. "And what may I create for you today? Something that will tantalize and delight your discerning taste buds?"

"We will have two of your burgers." Quinn winced at his order, feeling embarrassed to come to a Michelin Star restaurant to only order burgers.

"Excellent, I will handcraft them myself and bring out your certificates, of course." Henri bowed and left them alone.

"I can feel your judgment all the way over here." Markus urbanely laid the napkin on his lap and waited while an attendant poured water into their glasses. "I'll have a whisky, neat, and the lady will have a mimosa while we wait. And before you go, can you please enlighten her to what makes this burger so special?"

"Yes, sir. The burger is made from wagyu beef with black truffle and a seared foie gras. It is served with a jus made from the 1943 Bordeaux of which you will also get a comple-mentary bottle for the table. The bun and burger patty are covered entirely in edible gold." The waiter looked to Markus to see if he had completed his explanation to Markus's satisfaction.

"Are you able to tell the lady the price?"

"It costs five thousand dollars and you get a certificate signed by Henri with your burger number."

"That will be all." Markus waved him away, glancing at Quinn over the rim of his water glass, gauging her reaction.

"So how much is the poo the next day worth?" Quinn asked coolly, taking her own sip of water.

Markus laughed heartily. "And just when I thought I could impress you."

Once the burger arrived, it really was a thing of beauty. The gold leaf gave the impression that it was a work of art rather than a culinary delight. Quinn stared down at her plate while Henri grandly presented their certificates and joked with Markus. How on earth had her life changed so much that she was about to eat a five-thousand-dollar, gold-coated burger with a man she thoroughly detested, all in the name of her job?

The man in question seized the burger in his hands, the diamonds on the ring on his pinky finger glinting in the light, and took an enormous bite, the jus coating his lips. The same lips he smacked together appreciatively as he chewed with gusto. He paused, the burger midway to his mouth as he quirked a brow at her in askance.

"It does taste best while it's still warm."

Quinn took the burger, surprised at the smooth texture the gold gave it. *When in Rome...* She took a bite and the flavors exploded in her mouth, the sleek gold dissolving on her tongue. She could feel her eyes start to close as she savored the taste zinging across her taste buds. It was only when she remembered who sat across the table from her that she snapped them open, striving to appear bored.

But being a man who made his livelihood from reading other people's expressions, Markus wasn't fooled. "This is what money buys."

"It doesn't buy me." Quinn disdainfully wiped her hands on her napkin.

"We'll see."

~

"Hey, I'm surprised to see you having dinner here. I thought Mr Whale would be monopolizing your time." Kelly kicked her shoes off with relish as she entered their suite.

"Don't even joke about it," groaned Quinn, buttering her toast. After her five-thousand-dollar burger from earlier, she didn't have much of an appetite. "I told him I had a headache to escape. He's spending the night gambling, but I've had to organize a cabana for him tomorrow." Indignation made her cheeks burn. "Do you know he told me that I was expected to wear a bikini tomorrow and look the part?"

"You do know a lot of women wouldn't have a problem with getting paid to wear a bikini and hanging out poolside with a man who insists on spending ridiculous sums of money, right?" Kelly stole a piece of toast off Quinn's plate. Biting into it, she waited.

"Yeah, and there are names for that sort of bloody woman." Quinn put another piece of bread into the toaster. "I don't think I can do this. I can't handle being told that I have to do whatever he says just because he has money. I can't even stand being near him. He makes Lance look like a saint."

Kelly wiped a smear of butter from her downturned mouth. "Aww, you only have to get through another day. He leaves tomorrow evening."

Quinn felt like she wanted to cry. "And then what? What's the next one going to be like? If they're all like him, I'm serious, I can't do this."

Her friend put her arms sympathetically around her shoulders. "It'll get better, I promise. Anyway, it's like, three months till Christmas, and you love that. We'll go do Christmassy things and it'll be great, and everything will feel better."

Quinn glumly grabbed her toast from the machine. "I hope so. But I'm not sure how Christmassy a town fueled by gambling and bright lights is going to feel."

QUINN CHECKED the fruit platter before sending it over to where Markus reclined inside the cabana, surrounded by a bevy of bikini clad swimsuit-model wannabes downing the Cristal faster than she could get it delivered. From time to time, he would glance up at Quinn, probably to see if she was jealous. Personally, she was just glad she was relieved of the arrogant man's annoying presence.

Markus imperiously waved her over. Rolling her eyes skyward, she complied. "Yes, Markus, are you having a good time?"

"I would be if you'd done what I asked." He gestured dismissively at her attire, mouth compressed into a flat line, the other arm wrapped around a buxom companion.

Quinn glanced down at her outfit, a long-sleeved sun-smart shirt, wide-brimmed hat, lashings of neon pink zinc sunscreen and long board shorts. Widening her eyes innocently, she looked back at him. "You said to dress appropriately?"

"I didn't mean like someone's mom."

"Well, where I come from, we take our sun protection

very seriously." Quinn smiled, pleased that she'd outsmarted him. "Now, is there anything else I can help you with?"

"No, you can leave now. Arrange my car for six pm, and I expect you to accompany me to the airport."

"It will be my pleasure." Quinn didn't think she'd ever spoken truer words.

HER LEGS DEMURELY CROSSED, Quinn sat on the plush leather of the seat, watching the city vista flash past. Her heart accelerated at the thought of being rid of her obnoxious guest, a smile blooming on her face. She had a few days free till her next high roller guest, and she was looking forward to returning to being Kelly's assistant.

"I hope that smile is for me." Markus glanced up from his tablet, his lips quirking.

"Nope. Well, actually, a little bit."

"I hope I've left an impression on you. I know you certainly have on me." He reached into his coat and pulled out a blue box. "This is for you in appreciation for your time and effort for my stay." He handed it over.

Quinn hesitated. It didn't feel right to accept a gift from someone she loathed. "The Chimera's management compensates me adequately for the job and, obviously, you covered some quite expensive experiences for me while you stayed with us."

"Just take it. Consider it the last request of my stay." Markus's eyes narrowed while she spoke.

Quinn sighed, hesitantly opening the box. Inside lay an exquisite, delicate chain bracelet with a silver and gemstone bee charm. "Thank you. It really is lovely."

"Good," Markus brusquely said. "It reminded me of you. Such a busy little bee." The car pulled to a stop. "Quinn, I will be back. Don't think you can get rid of me that easily." The chauffeur opened the door, and Markus leaned in closer. "I believe the odds are in my favor." With a final smirk, he was gone, leaving Quinn afraid that he was delusional enough to actually believe they were.

CHAPTER 9

There were two things that struck Quinn when she met the glass artist the next morning with Kelly—her large periwinkle blue eyes and slender elegant shape of her hands, notwithstanding the callouses and burns on them. There was a warmth to her that drew a person in. Quinn liked her immediately. Evelyn Hart, the famed glass worker, had been commissioned to work on a large wall piece for the entrance to the theater. Quinn stood beside Kelly as Evelyn took measurements, photos and just generally stalked the space taking notes.

"Is this entire space available for my work?" she asked as she paced.

"Yes, as long as thoroughfares are kept clear," Kelly respectfully replied. It was clear that she was just as mesmerized by their visitor as Quinn was.

"I should be able to have some preliminary sketches back to you in a month's time. By the time we go back and forth with negotiations and fine tuning the design, it will be Christmas. I won't start fabrication till the new year." Evelyn finally stopped her roaming to return to the other women.

"Do you have plans for Christmas?" Quinn asked curiously.

Evelyn's entire face broke into an enormous smile. "Yeah, I'm going to Texas to visit my best friend who lives there with her brother. Our other best friend who lives in New York is coming as well. We've been best friends since high school, and we try to meet up several times a year, but it just seems like life keeps getting busier and busier and we don't find the time like we used to. But this year, this year we're making it happen." She peered at Quinn inquisitively. "How about you?"

"Well, we haven't been here long enough to get more than a week or so off and that's not really enough time to fly all the way back to Australia." Quinn sighed glumly. "I don't have any plans, really, and that sucks. Christmas has always been one of my favorite times of the year."

"I'm sure we'll figure something out as it gets closer," Kelly reassured her.

"I hope so," Quinn replied forlornly. "I really hope so."

THE WEEKS FLEW BY, and Kelly was right. Most of the high rollers that Quinn hosted were either nice or, for the most part, ignored her except to get her to arrange things for them. All in all, she was beginning to think she would be able to do the job after all. Today, she was to host another high roller and his wife. Julie hadn't been able to provide much information other than he hadn't been to the casino in months and she'd never met the wife.

Quinn strode around the high roller suite, making sure everything was perfect. She ran a finger along the edge of the window, peering down at it with satisfaction when no traces of dust appeared. The floral arrangements of orchids and bamboo were fresh. Her phone buzzed insistently. "Hello, Julie."

"Hey, Bob called, and he said that the Delaney's will be arriving in five minutes."

"Okay, I'll be right down." After a quick inspection of her appearance, she only made it to the front desk with seconds to spare. The sleek limousine glided to a stop, and the valet promptly opened the door. An older gentleman, his chestnut-colored hair silvered at the temple, stepped out, smiling at her in greeting before extending his hand back into the car to help his wife out. She was obviously much younger, a little on the plump side with twinkling, happy eyes.

"Hello, Mr and Mrs Delaney. I'm Quinn Williamson, and I'll be your hostess for your stay."

"Please, call me Steve." Steve wrapped a loving arm around his wife.

"And I much prefer Faith," his wife agreed, smiling up at him. "We're not terribly formal."

Quinn smiled warmly at them. "Well, Steve and Faith, if you would like to come with me, I'll escort you up to your suite and make sure you get settled in with everything you need." She had to stop herself from humming happily as she led the way to the elevator. She was going to enjoy looking after this lovely couple. Once upstairs, she showed them around and explained how various systems in the room worked and gave them her direct number for any requests.

"Quinn, I actually have a few, if you don't mind," Steve said quietly when his wife left the room to powder her nose.

"Anything."

"Can you organize a helicopter flight to Red Rock Canyon for some sunset champagne this evening? Faith hasn't been out much lately, and I want to spoil her."

"Of course. I'll make the arrangements straight away and liaise directly with you. Am I right in assuming you don't want Mrs Delaney to know?" Quinn kept her voice low for fear of being overheard.

Steve smiled gratefully at his co-conspirator. "Yes, you would be correct. Also, tomorrow, I aim to spend a fair chunk of my day at the tables. Would you be able to keep Faith company, maybe lunch and shopping, or she likes day spas?"

"It would be my pleasure. I can arrange an itinerary and send it through for your approval."

"That won't be necessary. I plan to be at the tables by nine am. If you could be up here before I leave, it would be appreciated."

"Of course. I'll send through details of your flight this evening and if there is anything else you require, you have my number." Quinn discreetly left the room, excited for the next few days. Every time a new high roller came to town, it felt like going on a first date, and lately they hadn't been great. Mostly boring, which, in her books, was still better than obnoxious. Wait till she told Kelly she got to spend the day going shopping tomorrow.

Quinn thought that Steve and Faith were just the most gorgeous couple she'd ever seen inhabit the high roller's suite. To be fair, most of the time it was a guy flashing his cash around and bringing up whatever bimbo he could find or pay for. She watched discreetly as Steve gave Faith a tender kiss, promising that she would have a fun day and then, with a brief nod to Quinn, left the room. Maybe it was a cowboy thing, but the only other ones she'd had dealings with had been complete gentlemen and in Luciano's case, the same as Steve, a complete marshmallow as far as his wife had been. A whisper of a thought wormed its way into her mind. *Would Jackson be like that with the woman he loved?*

"Steve has asked me to organize a few things for today. Is there anything in particular you would like to do?" Quinn asked as Faith gathered up her things.

"The big thing is I want to make sure I buy Christmas presents for everyone while I'm here." Faith's big eyes sparkled with excitement. "I have three strapping stepsons, a baby girl and one spoiled husband to buy for."

Quinn felt herself get caught up in the other woman's anticipation. "I think we can find something for them. If you're ready, we can start with that."

"I hope you had a good breakfast. My husband often says shopping is one of my superpowers."

Quinn laughed. "I'm up to the challenge." Opening the door, she gestured for Faith to precede her. "Or at least, I'll give it everything I've got."

Several hours later, Quinn was forced to concede that, even with her best intentions, her stamina for shopping was substantially less than Faith's. Her feet ached, and she was more than happy to sit down at the restaurant she'd reserved for them. Sore body parts aside, she'd had a blast. Her companion's energy was such a pleasure to be around. It was refreshing after the guests she'd had previously.

Quinn smiled as she watched her look through her shopping bags, checking over her purchases. "I think you did pretty well, all things considered. Remind me never to bargain with you. I'm bloody sure I'd lose."

Faith blushed a little under her praise. "That's what comes from running a cattle ranch. I was such a shy little mouse of a thing when I first moved there. I'm sure the triplets didn't even know I was there most of the time and they were such big boys even at twelve—and loud. Oh, my Lord, I'd never been in such a noisy house before. I've come a long way since then, I'm Mom to those boys now and my baby girl." Her smile slipped from her face and she looked teary. "I'm sorry. Since I've had my baby, I haven't been apart from her. I'm actually missing her a bit."

"I bet. From the photo you showed me earlier, she looks like a real cutie. Are her brothers looking after her?"

"One of them is. He stayed on the ranch and is so good with her. His other brother joined the military and the other is at medical school becoming a doctor. I know she is in good hands, and we are only going to be away for a few days, but..." Her voice trailed off.

"But you still miss your baby," Quinn finished for her. "You'll be home soon, and with these gorgeous presents you bought for everyone, too."

"Steve always wants me to wait until December to put up the tree and decorate the house. Every year, I sneak it forward a little. So far, I've managed to get it to mid-November. I can't help myself. I love Christmas and want it to last for as long as possible."

Quinn smiled as the waiter filled their glasses. "I love it, too."

"What are your plans this year?"

"I don't really have anything organized yet. Kelly and I are still fairly new in town." Quinn was beginning to think everyone had Christmas plans except her, which kind of sucked. "But I'd love to hear all about yours. Then eat up, I have an afternoon booked for us at the most exclusive day spa in Las Vegas."

"Well, I start making my Christmas puddings early, and I always make Steve and the boys pick the biggest tree they can find." Quinn settled in her chair, feeling slightly jealous of how lovely and cozy it all sounded. Idly, she wondered when her Christmas spirit was going to kick in. She reached for her glass of wine. At least she always had this sort of spirit to fall back on.

The next day as she bid them farewell, Quinn felt like she was saying goodbye to a long-lost friend. She found herself repeating several times to make sure that they made their visits to The Chimera a little more regular now that baby Allie was getting older. Just before she got into the car, Faith gave her a hug and whispered into her ear, "I hope you have a lovely Christmas." And with a final wave, she let her husband seat her in the car.

Quinn stood on the curb, waving until the limo pulled out into traffic and disappeared from sight. Heaving a sigh and feeling better for having met them both, she walked slowly back inside.

"Quinn," Julie called, waving her over.

"Yes, don't tell me I have a new high roller coming in today." Quinn didn't know if she was emotionally ready for another one.

"Not today. Housekeeping just called. They're on their way down now. There was something left in the room for you."

Quinn looked at Julie curiously, not a clue what it could be. She stared down at the large box before opening the little card attached.

Dear Quinn

Thank you for your kindness during my stay. I hope you enjoy this little present as much as I enjoyed buying it for you. I had to be sneaky so you didn't see me buy it. Merry Christmas, my friend.

Faith

The words blurred on the paper as tears swam in Quinn's eyes. She found herself overcome with emotion at the simple yet profound words.

"Well, are you going to open it?" Julie demanded.

Quinn looked at it hesitantly, scrunching her face. "It's a

Christmas gift. Maybe I should wait and put it under the tree when I get one?"

"When are you going to get one of those? Go on, open it." Not needing more encouragement, she opened the box to swathes of tissue paper and the smell of expensive leather. With reverent hands, she gently lifted out the highly sought-after handbag. "Oh my gosh, is that a—?" Julie asked in awe.

Quinn stared at it incredulously. "Yes, it is," she breathed.

"Some girls get all the luck. You got paid to go shopping and to the spa with her, and then she gives you this. I need to get out from behind this desk and be a hostess."

"Yeah, you say that now. But for every Faith, you need to deal with a hundred Markuses." And wasn't that the truth of the matter.

CHAPTER 10

The numbers leapt off the page of the calendar at Quinn. The first of November. *Oh my gosh, it's less than two months till Christmas.* Has it really been that long since she'd met the cowboy who still haunted her dreams? Quinn thought of Faith getting excited that she would soon be setting up her Christmas tree. Much safer to turn her mind to her new friend than something who was never meant to be. She smiled as she looked down at the handbag she'd been gifted from her as she waited for her next guest. This one was a little different. Instead of it being the usual high roller, this one was an extremely wealthy business-woman who was hosting a charity event for an animal adoption charity that Kelly was also helping coordinate.

The main conference room had been turned into a pet's paradise and a large pond had been installed with koi swimming languidly in its calm waters. There had been a kitten enclosure built around a luxurious lounging area where the attendees could cuddle a kitten while sipping a decadent cocktail. Personally, Quinn liked the dog walk that had been arranged to take place during the evening.

Quinn returned to the present just in time to see Randy greet their latest guest and point in her direction. Swiftly, Quinn stepped forward to greet her. "Misty Lewis? It's a pleasure to meet you. I'm Quinn, Kelly's assistant and your hostess for your stay."

Soft brown eyes smiled up at her, dimples dancing on her cheeks. "Hi, Quinn. I think you'll find that I'm not that much trouble to look after."

"That's good, because some of the kittens tried to escape this morning."

Misty giggled, quickly covering her mouth. "I'm sorry, that isn't funny."

Quinn rolled her eyes. "It's okay, I'd laugh too. Chora asked me to let you know that she's in the theater room checking that the animals are okay."

"That sounds like Chora. You've obviously met her. Do you think I thought I would find her anywhere else but with the animals?"

Quinn smiled in agreeance. The director of the Animals Are Forever charity had to be, without a doubt, one of the most passionate people she'd met in regard to the animals in her care. "No, I wouldn't imagine you would."

"I better not keep her waiting. Let's head over there first and make sure everything is under control, which I assume it is, given the lengthy and very comprehensive emails I've been receiving from Kelly."

A short brisk walk brought them to their destination, Quinn enjoying the appreciative silence the décor caused Misty. "Oh my. Your people have done wonders."

"Thank you. We try." Quinn scanned the room. No sign of Kelly. She assumed she was doing something behind the scenes before alighting on Chora's honey-blonde head. "I see Chora over there at the cat lounge."

Misty shook her head in amazement. "Cat lounge. What a

marvelous concept." She strode off in that direction, leaving Quinn to quickly follow in her wake.

Chora was sitting cross-legged on the floor, a puddle of kittens in her lap. "Hey, Misty. How was your flight?"

"Not too bad. That's one of the perks of having a private plane—you very rarely get a bad one." Quinn did a quick double take of her guest. Sure, she knew she was wealthy to warrant having her as a hostess, but she just seemed so, well, normal. "I see you have the kittens wrangled."

"They are an easy crowd to please. It's that one over there that doesn't want to know anything about me."

Chora pointed to what was the biggest cat Quinn had ever seen. In fact, she'd seen a lot of dogs that were smaller. Dramatic yellow eyes glared out from a black furred face, complemented by a smoky gray mane. The dark ears had little tufts of fur standing up from its tips. The overall impression was of regal indifference to the rubble it surveyed.

"Seriously, that is a huge cat. What breed is it?" Quinn asked.

"Duchess, named for her obvious snotty qualities, is a Maine Coon. A cat that has no right for such a judgmental attitude when she's knocked up and won't tell anyone who the father is." Chora shook her head in mock despair at the majestic cat.

"She looks like a pedigree cat. Is she one that you're hoping to adopt?" Quinn asked.

"It's a common misconception that animals who end up in shelters are ill-bred strays. I would say that someone paid a lot of money for her, and she's a prime example of people not taking responsibility and getting their pets fixed." Chora's voice rang with passion.

Duchess watched unblinkingly at Quinn's cautious approach. Gingerly, she knelt down, the cat continuing to maintain steady eye contact as she reached a hand out to stroke her soft fur. Emboldened when the cat didn't launch into an attack, she continued her administrations, Duchess closing her eyes in enjoyment.

"I think you've made a friend there," Chora said. "And believe me, that's something big. Duchess isn't really into making friends, which is why it's been so hard to get her adopted. Well, that and a belly full of babies." Chora shook her head again at the cat.

"Well, I think she's lovely." Quinn looked up to find the other women staring at her. "What?"

"At the shelter, we have a saying that people come in and they think they're the ones who pick the pet, but it's always the other way round. Congratulations, you've been adopted." Chora smiled proudly at her.

Quinn felt her mouth drop open. "Um, I live here at the casino. I'm pretty sure they have a bloody strict policy on pets. Doubly that if they're pregnant." She looked down regretfully at the blissfully purring cat. "I mean, she's lovely and all."

There was something to Misty's determined gaze that made Quinn begin to feel nervous. "But you like her?" she insisted.

"Yeah, but as I said, I live here." Quinn shrugged her shoulders at the impossibility of it all.

"Hmm." Misty refocused on Chora. "If everything is under control here, I'm going to go to my room to freshen up and go grab a bite to eat. I need to go over my notes for tonight, too." She raised her eyebrows to where Quinn sat with the still purring Duchess. "I need to make some phone calls as well."

Quinn wasn't sure why the way she said it made her feel so uneasy.

~

"MY BEST FRIEND was here not so long ago," Misty said around a mouthful of sushi. "She's doing an installation."

Quinn racked her brain for any tradesmen who might have come through. She knew that some new lights had recently been installed, but nothing else came to mind. "Um, I don't really have much to do with repairs that happen here."

"She doesn't do repairs. She's an artist. The Chimera has engaged her to create a glass installation." Misty looked at her like she was daft.

Understanding blossomed through Quinn. "Oh, you're friends with Evelyn Hart?"

"Yeah. After tonight, I'll head back to New York to tie up a few loose ends and then I'll be off to spend Christmas with her and Indie in Texas. I can't wait." Misty picked up another piece of sushi and dipped it into a container of wasabi.

"Evelyn mentioned something about a best friend back there and another in New York. This other friend must be something special to have you both so excited to catch up with her."

Misty's face softened. "We've all been friends since high school. I love both of my besties. Evelyn was always going to be famous. You could tell when we were in school that she was going to do big things."

"It doesn't seem like you've done too bad for yourself."

Misty shrugged modestly as she bit into her sushi. "But Indie, there's no one else like her. She makes you feel good just by being around her. You know that saying about when someone lights up a room? Well, they could have written that just for her. I'm ridiculously excited to get to spend Christmas with my two best friends." She glanced down at her watch. "That reminds me, I need to make those calls now. I shouldn't need anything from you for the rest of the evening, but will you still have your phone on you just in case?"

Quinn didn't mind the sound of getting to spend the evening snuggled up on the sofa with a blanket in her pajamas and watching something on the television. "I always do. Good luck with tonight. I know it will be a success, and Kelly will be there to make sure everything runs smoothly."

"Thanks." She picked up her phone. "Now, skedaddle."

"MISS LEWIS SAID I was to bring this up to you." The porter rolled in the trolley, a large pet container and box on it.

Quinn peered into the box to find a familiar black furry face glaring out at her. Alarm shot through her. Hadn't she made herself clear that she was in no position to be Duchess's new owner? She was sure she'd mentioned it once or twice. "I think she's made some sort of mistake."

"She said you might say that and said to give this to you." He handed her an envelope and waited expectantly for her to read it.

Duchess needs a special home, and I think you're the one to give it to her. Don't worry, I've okayed it with Lachlan. There was no way he was going to say no to me.

Misty (gifter of cats)

Quinn looked down in disbelief at her new, pregnant cat. Still in her cage, Duchess licked her paw, completely under-whelmed by her change in circumstances.

"I KNOW you have to do everything in your power to please the client, but this is where I draw the line." Kelly, hands on hips, glared down at Duchess. Duchess, for her part, stared out into the distance, refusing to acknowledge her.

"So, you draw the line at a cat, but not when I'm forced to go on dates with obnoxious whales?" Quinn stared incredulously back at her friend. "You do hear yourself, right?"

Kelly had the grace to look ashamed. "Okay, but this thing is nothing but a giant furball. I mean, she's huge and a little on the fat side."

"I'll brush her every day to keep the fur down, and she's not fat. She's pregnant."

"What!?" screeched Kelly, her voice raising up the octaves dramatically. "No way. I'm not having kittens in this apartment."

"Misty got Lachlan to sign off on it and you know how much of a stickler he is for keeping our VIP guests happy." Quinn took a great deal of satisfaction in watching Kelly chew on that for a while.

"I'm going to have to invest in a lint roller, aren't I?" Kelly admitted defeat.

"Probably. And maybe a pet vacuum." Quinn settled down beside Duchess and wrapped an arm around her new furry friend. Duchess leaned into her slightly, closing her eyes as she scratched her under the chin. "See? She's already settling in."

A slightly malicious smirk crossed Kelly's perfect features. "Oh, that reminds me." She slapped her forehead lightly. "Julie mentioned you have a new high roller to look after next week."

"Yeah, well that gives me a nice break to help Duchess feel at home and become friends."

"Don't you even want to know who it is?"

"You seem pretty keen to tell me, so it can't be good." Quinn leveled a flat look at Kelly, waiting for the axe to drop.

"Markus Jamison."

CHAPTER 11

The pillow hit Quinn on the face with a resounding thump. "Hey!" she bellowed, making Duchess give a complaining meow. "What was that for?"

Kelly grinned impishly at her, not the slightest bit remorseful. "I've been thinking, I'm sick of all the it-doesn't-really-feel-like-Christmas mooching. So, I'm going to do something about it. Get up, shower, feed the cat, and let's get going."

Duchess settled herself against Quinn's chest. "What do you think, girl?" she asked the cat as she stroked her head. "Should I do what mean old aunty Kelly says?" The feline cast a dirty look in Kelly's direction, causing a tinkle of laughter to explode from Quinn. "Looks like I'm spending the day in bed with my cat."

Kelly gave her a disgusted look. "Seriously, Quinn, you're too young to make a statement like that. Now get up. I've made plans."

"Fine," huffed Quinn. "They better be good."

"Well, we're going to do something each day till Markus

arrives. Then, obviously, you'll need to be at his beck and call, and then we'll do more all the way until Christmas." Kelly quirked a brow at her friend. "How do you feel about doing a marathon dressed as Santa Claus?"

"Um, can't say I've given it any bloody consideration."

"You might want to." With that final comment, Kelly waltzed from the room.

Quinn snuggled up to her cat for a moment—funny how quickly she'd taken to feeling like Duchess was hers—and whispered into the snoozing feline's ear. "I'm beginning to feel afraid." When no answer came from the creature, she sighed and headed for the shower.

THE SKATE SKIDDED on the slippery ice making Quinn give a cry of alarm. Where there had once been a water-filled pool, host to epic parties during the summer, now stood a glistening ice-skating rink—one that Quinn was doing her best to not topple over on. She had to give it to Kelly. The bar setup with hot cocoa and s'mores, the Christmas carols and the fairy light covered palm trees did go a long way to giving it a holiday feel.

Kelly effortlessly glided by, making Quinn want to pick up the penguin glider she clutched at for balance and throw it at her. "Are you in the fa-la-la-la-la mood yet?" Kelly's words floated back to her.

"I mean, I've never ice skated period, and certainly never on a frozen pool in a casino before. And ice skating is always one of those things they have in the holiday movies."

"And Christmas novels."

"And Christmas novels," Quinn agreed.

"Well, if this doesn't get you in the mood, I have another trick up my sleeve for tonight."

Quinn's skate dug into the ice again, making her cuss softly under her breath. "Yeah, what's that?"

"Put your shoes back on and grab a hot cocoa, and then we'll go find out." With a little swoosh, Kelly glided over to the side of the rink, glancing impatiently over her shoulder for Quinn to follow. Muttering under her breath, Quinn slipped and skidded her way to follow suit.

Next up on the agenda was something Quinn had never experienced before—driving around a racing track. Every square inch of the speedway was decked out in festive lights. Nativity scenes, shooting stars, Santas climbing down chimneys, reindeer, and everything in between. Loud carols blasted over the sound system as Kelly and Quinn slowly drove around the track.

"Now, this screams Christmas, don't you think?" Kelly asked as she peered out her window.

"You can't mistake it for having a Christmas theme," Quinn agreed, wondering just how big the electricity bill for the light display was.

Kelly popped her head back inside the car. "I'm beginning to think you're still not getting into the Christmas spirit."

"Not yet." It wasn't like Quinn didn't want to be. She did, wholeheartedly. But none of what they had done so far had given her that special happiness that only the festive season could. Sure, she'd appreciated the effort and spectacle that had gone into it all, but something felt off somehow.

"I got you." Kelly didn't seem the least bit perturbed. "Tomorrow, after work, I have some more ideas and then, on our day off, you just wait."

And true to her word, Kelly tried hard. The Christmas display in a rival casino was done on such a grand scale that it boggled Quinn's mind at the effort that had gone into creating it. She thought the carolers were a nice touch, as was the fake snow that drifted down from the roof every thirty minutes. And she'd never seen a wetsuit clad Santa feeding sharks before—that definitely scored bonus points for originality. Quinn guessed that even sharks were entitled to have Christmas treats as well.

But even though the sharks didn't do the trick, Kelly wasn't to be discouraged. As promised, on their day off, she had one final ace up her sleeve.

"Are you going to tell me where we're going?" Quinn asked for what felt like the hundredth time.

"I did." Kelly indicated as she turned onto the highway, leaving the bright lights of The Strip behind them.

"You told me to dress warm. You didn't actually tell me where we're going," grumbled Quinn.

"Near enough." Unfazed by her friend's whining, Kelly turned up the music and continued on her merry little way. After a while, there were only random houses set amongst rocky landscapes, the mountains that had been in the distance now rearing up in front of them.

"Are we going to Mount Charleston? Are you taking me to see real snow?" Quinn leaned forward to peer out the windscreen, her excitement threatening to bubble over. "You are, aren't you?"

Kelly laughed. "This is the most animated I've seen you in ages about Christmas. Yes, we're going to go see snow."

The remainder of the trip felt like it trickled by, but the mountains steadily grew until they were at the base of them and on their way up. Quinn gave a little squeal of delight, spying the first pocket of snow on the side of the road. "Oh my gosh, Kelly, I see white stuff."

A little further along, Kelly pulled the car over and both girls exited, Quinn slipping and sliding her way as she explored. She couldn't resist reaching down and grabbing a handful of it, marveling at how cold and wet it was. It felt surreal to be up here surrounded by nature when an hour ago they'd been in the heart of Sin City. She clomped back to where Kelly had magically produced a thermos and was leaning against the warmth of the side of the car's hood. She gratefully accepted a cup of hot cocoa and idly stared down at the swirling brown goodness, the shades mingling together as steam rose comfortingly from it. Quinn felt like her thoughts and the drinks had quite a bit in common.

"I'm sorry if I've been a pain in the bum," she began, searching for the right words. "It's just been really hard getting into the holiday mood. I think maybe because back down there"—she whirled her hand vaguely in the direction they'd come from—"it all seems so artificial and materialistic. I mean, look at my job. My sole task is to make sure that rich people are happy and remain happy so they will continue to spend their money at The Chimera." She took a bracing sip, luxuriating in the slide of delicious warmth as it flowed down into her belly. "I don't think the crummy Christmas I had last year is helping either, and then there's all the fallout afterwards when I broke up with Lance." She smiled sadly at Kelly. "But being up here … I don't know, maybe it's because this is the closest I've ever been to a white Christmas before. Maybe it's the sense of space and tranquility. I feel like I have a sense of peace that I've been missing lately."

Kelly stared reflectively off into the distance. "Last Christmas wasn't all bad. You did get to meet a very cute cowboy." She winked at her friend.

With a jolt, Quinn remembered that it had been nearly a year since she'd met Jackson and had indirectly been sent on the path she currently walked. Sometimes when she was forced to politely smile at whichever high roller was in her care, her mind would drift to the tall Colorado cowboy and wonder if he ever thought of her too. "It's strange, I still think about him. For one moment, I got to meet him, and I think that was all it was meant to be. Anyway, I was with Lance then, it wasn't like anything was going to happen. All we did was talk a couple of times."

Kelly looked shrewdly over the rim of the cup clasped tightly between her gloved hands. "But if you hadn't been with Lance?"

"It doesn't matter now. Anyway, a nice guy like that, cute as anything? He probably has a girlfriend by now."

Kelly pushed herself off the car. "Maybe. But if you've had enough of this cold, wet stuff, can we please get back in the car where I can warm up?"

Quinn gave a final glance around, breathing in the fresh alpine air before nodding. As they drove back down the mountain, she found herself more centered. She wasn't sure what was the cause—the snow, the mountain air, or thinking about a humble cowboy who had briefly walked into her life before leaving one heck of an impression on the way out.

LATER AS SHE CUDDLED DUCHESS, the cat vibrating against her hand as Quinn stroked her lush fur, purrs low and fluttering emanating from the feline, her mind drifted again to the Colorado cowboy. In the background, she could hear Kelly muttering about cat hair and attacking the sofa armed with a lint roller and vacuum. Jackson had been so looking forward to spending Christmas back at the ranch with his family last year. She wondered if he would be bringing a special someone with him this year. She gave Duchess a little kiss on top of her head.

"Don't worry, girl. We can spend Christmas together eating turkey and ham. I might even be able to steal some pastries from Marie and we can really celebrate in style."

Quinn looked at Duchess's rounded sides. "That's if you haven't made me a grandmother by then."

Duchess didn't even bother opening her eyes, her low rumbling soothing as Quinn escaped to a fantasy of snow-covered Colorado peaks and nice cowboys.

CHAPTER 12

The arches of her feet screamed for release from the agony they were in. If Quinn had known how much of the day she'd be standing motionless beside the velvet-covered table, she'd have reconsidered her choice of footwear. Since Markus had arrived that morning and smiled smugly at her and snapped his fingers, she'd been forced to be at his side. The only saving grace was that he was only here for the day. That evening he would jet off to Macau, China. Maybe, if Quinn was lucky, he might even find love while he was over there. She sourly smiled at him when he won another hand, wondering how much he needed to win before he'd leave. Probably a great deal based on the stack of chips in front of him.

She wiggled her toes again and wondered what Jackson would be doing tonight. In her mind, she could see him stepping out into the bright lights, waving to the crowd as he had in Brisbane. Quinn could see him standing tall amongst his fellow bull riders, confident in his ability to tame the beast... An insistent tapping on her arm brought her sharply back to reality.

"Quinn, you can stop daydreaming about me. The real thing is right in front of you." Markus smirked to the rest of the table, guffaws greeting his wit. Quinn shot daggers at him, plastering a brittle smile on her face as she tilted her head at him.

"Markus, I believe I was smiling while I was daydreaming, which quite obviously meant it had nothing to do with you." More chuckles sounded but were quickly stifled as Markus glared at them.

He gestured for an attendant to see to his winnings and stood, buttoning his jacket closed. "I think I've played all I care to here." Quinn sighed when she saw the look she was on the receiving end of from Eddie. She wondered how long it would take to get to Lachlan. "Gentlemen, a pleasure as always."

"A pleasure taking our money, don't you mean?" one of the other gamblers grumbled. Markus accepted the observation as his due and held out his arm for Quinn.

Not long now. Just grin and bear it. Knowing refusing was futile, she accepted and allowed him to escort her from the room.

"I know I have not been able to give you the attention that you crave from me," Markus said smoothly as they traversed the corridor. "But I'll be back in a couple of days and, as a surprise for you, I've already arranged for you to have time off and I'll give you a Christmas you'll never forget."

Quinn's eyes narrowed at his high-handed manner and the fact that Lachlan had sold her off yet again. "It's such a shame no one mentioned it to me. I've made other plans."

A dark expression turned his eyes mean. "Cancel them."

"No."

"I'm not a man used to hearing that."

"Then get used to it. I've been honest with you from the start. I'm not interested in you. And before you twist it all up in your head, it's not some sort of denying my feelings or playing hard to get. I find you a disgusting human being and loathe being around you. You use your money to manipulate people, and there is no chance I'm going to ruin my Christmas by being forced to be with you." Quinn held her head high, glaring down her nose at him. "Your limo will be picking you up in an hour. If that is all you require from me, I have better things to do with my job than stand around like some sort of trophy for a man like you."

Spine ramrod straight, she went to walk away but Markus didn't release the grip on her arm. He leaned in close, making a show of inhaling her perfume from her neck. Quinn grimaced, hating his closeness to her. "Quinn, I'll be back. And you better be ready to leave with me."

She glared at him from the corner of her eye and, feeling the pressure release on her arm, marched off, determined not to let him see how much he'd rattled her.

~

"Seriously, Kelly, I don't know what else to do. If this was happening in my private life, I'd be tempted to get a restraining order against him." Quinn dangled the toy in front of Duchess, the pregnant cat swatting at it vigorously with her paw. She looked over to where her friend was glued to her tablet. "Kelly, are you even listening to me?"

"Huh?"

"That's what I thought." Quinn tossed the toy to Duchess and stood up. "What has you so interested?" She tried to peer over her friend's shoulder, Kelly quickly closing the screen. *What on earth?*

"Look, I'm sorry you had such a bad day. I listened enough to know that." Kelly scrunched up her face teasingly and then smiled at Quinn. "Do you want to do something tomorrow? I have the day off and I didn't see any bookings for VIPs that you need to host."

The thought of having a well-deserved girls' day with Kelly did sound appealing… "What did you have in mind?"

"I'm not sure yet. But trust me, when I figure it out, I know you're going to love it."

Quinn looked suspiciously at Kelly and then shrugged her shoulders in acceptance. It would beat sitting around in their suite all day. "Okay. What have I got to lose?"

"Not a thing, Quinn. Who knows? You might even gain something."

A thrill of anticipation shivered up Quinn's spine, and she immediately felt silly for the reaction to such vague words. Maybe it was because she'd been wound so tight all day dealing with Markus. What she really needed was a long soak in a nice hot bath, a glass of wine and a good book to read. Yep, that was the answer. And giving her friend one last appraising glance, she departed to do just that.

IT CAME as a surprise to Quinn that she'd been living in Las Vegas for a few months now and had never made it to the Thomas and Mack Center. And from the signage, it looked as though a rodeo was in town.

"Did you know about this?" she demanded.

Kelly appeared to be engrossed with finding them a park. "Yep."

"And this is your plan for today?"

"Ooh, there's a spot over there." Kelly jumped on the vacant park and switched off the ignition. Finally, she made eye contact with Quinn. "I might have found out yesterday that the NFR finals was coming to town. And I might have asked my contacts to find out if Jackson would be here."

For a moment, Quinn was robbed of breath, the sound of her heart pounding unnaturally loud in her ears. "And is he?"

"Yeah. Look, Quinn"—Kelly reached out and grabbed her hands—"I don't know where he is going to be, but don't you think it's worth a shot to try?"

Quinn's thoughts scattered like leaves on the wind. She didn't know what to think. The mere mention of Jackson was enough to make her pulse race. "Kelly, I appreciate you trying. But as you said, we don't even know where he's going to be. Not to mention that, if we did find him, he might have a girlfriend by now."

"I checked. His current status on his bull rider athlete's profile is single."

Quinn's mouth went dry. Everything in her wanted to run to the door and find him, to see if he even remembered her. "I guess it would be rude not to try after you went to all this effort and everything."

"Does that mean we're going on a cowboy hunt?"

"Let's go get them, Tex."

Quinn's confidence quickly dissipated like fog on a cool morning when she stepped inside and saw the sheer volume of people milling around. Her only previous experience had been her first rodeo, but this was so far next level it was like another universe. Feeling her stomach drop, she turned to Kelly.

"Even if Cupid was on our side and he's actually here, with this many people, there's no way it's going to work." She gestured around her. "There are literally thousands of cowboys here. Like we're ever going to accidently run into him."

Kelly's eyes went wide with shock. Mutely, she grabbed Quinn's arm and gestured out into the crowd. "Um, Quinn?" In slow motion, like the parting of the red sea, a gap formed in the dense pack in front of them, allowing them a brief glimpse of a tall, broad-shouldered, golden-haired cowboy. Jackson. Quinn's knees went weak at Cupid's accuracy.

FROM HIS HEIGHT, Jackson was able to see over the crowd. A flash of sandy-brown hair captured his attention, causing his heart to leap. He thought of all the sandy-haired slender women he'd seen in the crowds since he'd met the Australian who had stuck in his mind. In the year since, she'd never been far from his thoughts and he'd often thought of her as he drove to another event, worried about whether or not she was being treated right by that douche of a boyfriend who didn't deserve her.

Instinctively, he looked again, this time the crowd parting enough for him to catch sight of the two women looking lost in the crowd. The sandy-haired woman still had her back turned to him, but her blonde companion was facing him, anxiously scanning the crowds. There was something familiar about her. Their eyes met, and his blood began to pound furiously in hope. The blonde began to gesture animatedly, trying to get her friend's attention. The blonde bore more than a passing resemblance to the PR lady of last year's Australian rodeo. Kelly. That was her name.

It had to be her. Unbidden, his feet began to propel him forward as the brunette slowly turned at her friend's urging. That face—the one that had only visited in his dreams— gazed out across the crowd at him.

"Quinn?" He breathed her name like an incredulous prayer, the crowd melting into the background as long strides covered the ground between them. "Quinn." This time his heart cried it as loudly as his voice.

She beamed at him as recognition blossomed and, with light bouncy steps, she made her way quickly to meet him.

Her cheeks glowed as she stared up at him in wonderment. "Jackson? Is it really you?"

He thought his heart would stop at the way she looked at him—a way that he had only dared hope she would if they ever were to meet again. "It is." He laughed. Now that he had her in front of him, he didn't know what to do. "What are you doing here?"

"Kelly got a job here in Las Vegas"—she flicked a grin to her blonde friend who was grinning like a Cheshire cat —"and she said she wouldn't take it unless I came too. So, I'm working as her assistant some of the time and as the high roller VIP hostess the rest."

"Did your boyfriend move, too?" Even mentioning that slimebag was enough to leave a sour taste in his mouth.

"No, we actually broke up not long after I met you." There was something in her look, the way she said it, that made his heart grasp to take hold of the thought that she might somehow feel something for him.

Her hazel eyes were enormous as she stared at him, freely roaming his face as if committing it to memory, or perhaps to compare it to one she already held fast to her heart. At least, that was what Jackson hoped.

"Guys," Kelly interrupted. "It's really noisy in here, and I think we're kinda in the way."

"I was on my way to get some lunch when I saw you"—he paused briefly before he remembered to include Kelly —"both," he finished lamely.

Kelly gave him an understanding smile as though she knew who his attention was focused on. "Look, I need to head back. I've got a few things that have been sent through as urgent." She gave Jackson a sly wink. "Do you think you could keep Quinn company? She hasn't had lunch either."

Jackson smothered a chuckle as Quinn turned horrified

at her friend's less-than-subtle attempt at matchmaking. "It would be my pleasure."

It was charming—the way her cheeks pinkened. It made her look, if possible, even prettier. "You don't have to if you have other plans," she stammered, eyes narrowing threateningly at Kelly.

He took his hat from his head and held it steadfastly over his heart. "I couldn't think of anyone I'd rather share a meal with." The way she indecisively bit down on her full lower lip distracted him, momentarily making him forget his train of thought.

"Well, then it would be rude not to accept." Her eyes brightened as she beamed up at him. For a moment, Jackson forgot how to breathe. If she kept looking at him like that over lunch, he was liable to forget to eat.

QUINN KNEW she'd been staring at Jackson as he spoke, but she couldn't help herself. She was quite simply transfixed by his presence. There was something solid, real, about him that made her feel anchored to him. He held her hand as they made their way through the press of people, a sea of cowboy hats and denim. Jackson's hold on her hand was her lifeline. If he let go, she was scared he would disappear into that ocean, never to surface again.

The hard planes of Jackson's back slammed into her face as she collided into him, a surprised "oof" escaping her. She'd been so caught up in her musing that she hadn't noticed him stopping. His glorious blue eyes twinkled down at her, a mixture of amusement and apology shining in them.

"I thought you might want to catch up with him," he said by way of explanation.

Mystified, she forced her face to relax, aware she'd

scrunched it up in a most unattractive manner. "Catch up with who?" She followed the direction of his gaze, scanning the crowd until she locked on to a waving dark-haired man with a slender blonde pushing a double stroller. The beaming smile could only belong to one person. "Luciano!" She waved excitedly back. It was impossible to not have a soft spot for the enthusiastic Brazilian bull rider.

Dodging several people, Jackson and Quinn made their way over, Luciano surprising her when he wrapped her in a gigantic bear hug, the greeting suitable for a long-lost relative. "Quinn, you have no idea how happy it makes my heart to see you again"—he gave a sly sideways glance up at the tall Colorado cowboy—"and with my good friend, Jackson, no less." Quinn knew her face was flaming as she gazed curiously at the woman beside Luciano, the famous Frankie she'd heard so much about the previous year. Luciano proudly wrapped his arm around his wife. "Quinn, this is my Querida, Frankie."

Frankie smiled warmly at her, her eyes twinkling with hidden mirth. "I believe I have you to thank for the drop bear I received last Christmas?"

Quinn had forgotten about that. She giggled, brushing some stray strands of hair from her face. "I didn't want him to disappoint you."

"He never disappoints. But when I found that in my Christmas stocking, I knew he had to have had some extra help."

"I'm sure you'll have plenty of time to catch up with the Navarro's later," Jackson said, looking in the direction they'd originally been headed. Quinn was caught by surprise at the implied possibility that Jackson assumed this wasn't the only time she was going to be there for a rodeo. "Quinn and I were on our way to get something to eat, if you guys will excuse us."

Luciano laughed heartily, Jackson sending him a level gaze. "Frankie," he said to his wife. "Do you remember what it was like to be freshly in love? I wanted to keep you to myself all the time, too."

Quinn shook her head in denial, bemused when Jackson reddened, muttering something at Luciano that she couldn't quite make out and then, with a quick wave, they were on their way again. She stared at Jackson's broad back as he towed her through the crowd, wondering what it was that he'd said. Her belly gave a funny little flip flop as, for the briefest of moments, she wondered if the Brazilian knew something she didn't. She shook her head, clearing it of that madness as they entered the food hall, Jackson pouncing on the first available table.

Later, after one of the best hot dogs she'd ever eaten and a chocolate sundae, Quinn was shocked to see that several hours had flown by. Somehow, even with the constantly changing people at the neighboring tables, she'd failed to register the length of time that had eclipsed as she'd sat with Jackson, each filling the other in with what had happened since they'd seen each other last.

Her heart had filled with pride when he'd told her how well his year had gone in the rankings. She'd listened when he'd talked lovingly about the previous Christmas, his family, and some changes that had happened at the ranch. For his part, he'd seemed extremely happy when she'd told him about the breakup with Lance, and less so when she'd briefly skimmed over the trouble that he'd then inflicted on her career.

"But without that, you wouldn't have moved to Las Vegas with Kelly for your jobs, and there would be no way that we'd been sitting across from each other having this conversation," Jackson had sagely noted.

"That's true. Kelly insisted I come with her because she

knew how hard Lance was making it for me," Quinn agreed. "The job has been bloody hectic and, at times, the guests are challenging." Her foot began to tap under the table as she thought about her next guest she'd be forced to deal with.

"Do you get many days off?" Eyes that would put spring skies to shame looked at her in concern.

"Sometimes we can work for weeks without a break, and then others we can get several days off at once. Like this week." Quinn forced her foot to cease its movement, irritated that Markus had ruined her lovely lunch with Jackson and he didn't even have to be there to do it. "I have a couple of days free and then I have a"—she searched for the best way to describe Markus Jamison—"fairly demanding and time-consuming high roller coming. And believe me, you would be amazed at what the casinos do to keep them happy. And this one isn't just a high roller. He's a whale."

Bemused blue eyes looked quizzically back at her. "Whale?"

"Gamblers that make high rollers look like they're frugal with their money."

Jackson reached across the table and lifted her hand, gently rubbing the back of her fingers with his thumb. The sensation of his callouses as his thumb moved rhythmically sent a shiver through her. She felt the heat creep up her face and knew she was blushing.

"I compete in the evenings, and most mornings it takes a while for the stiffness to wear off." Quinn bit her tongue, a very naughty image springing to mind. Catching her amusement, he snorted, exchanging a knowing look with her that quite clearly said he knew that her mind had ended up in the gutter. "I'm shocked at you, young lady. I'm talking about aches and pains from being knocked around by a royally annoyed bull. What I was trying to say, or ask really, was if you would like to spend some time together?"

Quinn licked her lips, her mouth suddenly dry as he regarded her steadily with his piercing blue eyes, and found she couldn't look away from his indecipherable expression. "I think I'd like that."

A lopsided smile adorned his lips in reply. "I think I'd like that, too."

CHAPTER 13

The car's engine was loud as it parked on her chest, the weight pinning her down as grass tickled her nose... *Wait, what kind of dream was she having?* Quinn forced her reluctant eyelids open to find glaring yellow eyes mere inches away. The demand was quite clear. *Human, where is my breakfast, and why are you still in bed?* She reached a hand out of the snug covers to run it gently down Duchess's blossoming sides, the skin twitching under the contact. Quinn could feel a squirming sensation beneath her hand.

"Not long now and then you're gonna be a mommy."

Quinn blissfully closed her eyes, a warm glow filling her soul when she thought about seeing Jackson again. She wasn't sure what she'd done right to deserve a second chance with him, but whatever happened, she was going to make sure she deserved the opportunity. A bop on her nose from a soft paw made her blink.

"Okay, Duchess, I'm getting up already. You do know that there's plenty of cat kibble out there, but no, nothing but the best for you." The cat didn't seem the least bit interested in her suggestion and, with a decidedly matronly wobble, walked to the edge of the bed, landing with a little grunt before padding out of the room.

"Just who I wanted to see," Kelly said as soon as Quinn set foot outside of her bedroom. Quinn winced at the annoyed tone and, just like that, *poof*, all her warm happy feelings dissipated.

"Can it wait till I have a cup of tea?"

"I wasn't talking to you. I was talking to her." Kelly glared down to where the completely uninterested Duchess was washing her back foot. Her friend grabbed a white skirt off the table and held it up accusingly to the feline. "What do you call this?" Duchess, for her part, chose not to engage in the conversation and continued with her grooming. Accepting she was not going to get satisfaction from that quarter, she held the garment out to Quinn. "Have you seen what your cat did?"

Quinn peered at the skirt, pretending not to see straight away what the issue was. A blind man could have spotted it. It looked like something—or some cat—had made a nest in the skirt, a thick covering of black fur left as evidence. At some point, the culprit must have felt unwell, because there also appeared to be residue of a cat's meal on it.

"Before you slander poor Duchess, you have no proof."

"I'm holding it in my hot little hand," Kelly spluttered indignantly, her face reddening. "I'm no CSI, but I'm pretty sure if I take a sample of the fur left at the crime scene and check it against one pregnant furball, it's gonna match."

"It's all circumstantial evidence." Quinn thought a vein was going to pop in Kelly's forehead. Deciding she had gone far enough, she raised her hand to calm her. "Look, I don't think it's fair to cast the blame around." She gestured for Kelly to settle when her friend looked like she was getting ready to fire up again. "But in the interest of continued goodwill in this household, I am willing to drop it off at the dry cleaners and get it taken care of for you."

Kelly took a deep, long-suffering sigh. "Fine. And for my part, I'm willing to let the matter go now that we've reached a resolution." As if clearing the matter from her mind, she smiled brightly at Quinn. "And as further compensation, you can tell me all about seeing Jackson again yesterday."

A giddy rush went through her. Where to even begin? "It was like I've known him forever, like we haven't not seen each other for a year." Hearing how silly it sounded now that she'd uttered it out loud, she self-consciously brought her hand to her mouth. "I don't know how to describe it without sounding stupid."

Kelly sighed dreamily. "I think it sounds lovely. You're a romantic and you always have been. I'm a bit more"—she rolled her eyes skyward as though casting her mind for the right description—"cynical."

"I think you're as soft as a marshmallow deep inside, you're just scared to let someone in. I'm really going to enjoy the day you fall in love."

"Never going to happen." Kelly threw a pillow, one that Quinn easily dodged. She loved her blonde-haired friend, but it saddened her that Kelly never let anyone in. As far as she knew, she was the only close friend Kelly possessed. Sometimes when she thought she was alone, Kelly would become silent, a haunting air of sadness hanging over her like fog over the marshes that Quinn had once seen in a book about Ireland.

"You're the worst thrower."

"Then stay still to make it easier for me." Kelly laughed, narrowing her eyes playfully like she was trying to size her up. "Now that you've met Jackson again and you're single this time, what's the next step?

"What do you mean?"

"Let me spell it out for you. What do you plan to do about it?"

And therein lay the crux of the problem. When it seemed like she was never going to see Jackson again, it had been easy to turn him into the fantasy—the perfect boyfriend who would never let her down. She didn't know if she was ready to give that up, to take a chance on having the illusion shattered by the possibility of a not-so-perfect reality.

"I like him, Kelly. But he's only here for a few days and maybe that's for the best."

Disappointment warred with disbelief across Kelly's polished features. "Hang on, let me get this straight. You get a second chance to let something happen between the two of you and now you don't want it to?"

Quinn's heart constricted just at the thought of letting this chance slip through her grasp. "It's not like that. Look, it doesn't even matter. I'm being silly. We did make plans for while he's in town."

Her friend smiled approvingly as she gently removed Duchess from settling on her pristine silk pajama pants. "Well, that's a start. What are you going to do?"

"Um, see the Christmas fountain show, maybe go ice skating and a few other things depending on if we get time," Quinn said softly, causing Kelly to strain forward to catch her murmured words.

"I thought it was all artificial?" Kelly's brows turned into dark slashes on her face as she glared her protest.

"It is, but I want Jackson to see it. He loves Christmas as much as I do, and I don't know, maybe that will make it special."

"Unbelievable. All I can say is enjoy your freedom while you still can. A certain whale is going to be in town soon and he's going to want all of your attention. I don't think Markus Jamison is the sharing kind of man."

~

EVERY BULL RIDER knows that the thrill of it, the heart-pounding, nerve-tingling adrenaline shot, is what made them want to do what most people thought was plumb crazy. It was addiction wrapped up in intoxication, and there was no way to stop the craving once you'd had a taste. Jackson was beginning to suspect that one Quinn Williamson was about to supplant it in his life. He'd quite simply never felt about anyone the way he did about this girl that so far, in one year, he had only spent a grand total of two-going-on-three days with. If one of his friends was telling him that it had happened to them, he'd have told them they were crazy.

He was still shaking his head over the ridiculousness of it all as he stood waiting in front of what appeared to be a food van selling cookie dough when his heart lurched, somehow recognizing her before his brain could even register the sight of her.

She was a sight, grown men's heads just about snapping off their necks as they whiplashed around to catch another glimpse of her. Her long hair shot through with ripples of caramel and honey framed her face and cascaded down her back, looking like it belonged in a shampoo commercial. Quinn wore tightly-fitted what looked to Jackson to be leather pants, a long body-hugging black top and a caramel floating sleeveless vest. As usual, she carried a monogramed bag with her, this one smaller than her usual one. The entire look was expensive and so far out of his reach it wasn't funny.

Jackson spared a glance down at his own attire—freshly pressed blue jeans, his good stepping out hat, recently cleaned boots, NFR official competitor's jacket and the blue button-up shirt his mom had told him made his eyes sparkle.

An insidious whisper of insecurity and doubt entered his thoughts.

"Hello, Jackson." Quinn gave him a hug and kissed his cheek. The polished greeting set him to clearing his throat and shuffling his feet. "You're looking refreshed today. It's your eyes or something."

Her own beautiful eyes were hidden behind large, dark sunglasses and Jackson began to pray that the sun would go behind the clouds so she would be forced to remove them and he would be afforded the opportunity to gaze deeply into the windows of her soul. "Thanks. Now, what have you got in store for us today? You didn't tell me anything yesterday about your plans," he said as he fell into step alongside her.

Quinn's small, cool hand slipped into his as if it were the most natural thing in the world to stroll, hand in hand, down The Las Vegas Strip together. "Well, I thought we could do some of the Christmas activities they have here since we met last year just before Christmas and now we've met again— and it's just before Christmas." Her cheeks pinkened as though she was embarrassed that she was making a big deal out of it.

"I've never done anything in this town except compete. I think it sounds great. Lead the way." Words he would regret sooner rather than later as he skidded awkwardly around the ice to her peals of laughter.

"I thought you were from Colorado?" she said between bouts of laughter.

"I am. But that doesn't mean I'm any good at skating." He held on to the side of the rink to gather his breath and balance, watching her own awkward progress. "From where I'm standing, you're not in a position to judge."

"But I'm from Australia. It's not like ice is a big thing for us, so I get a free pass. Maybe we should stop before you pull a muscle or something." Her eyes went huge at the thought, her gloved hands flying to her mouth. "Oh my gosh, Jackson. I'm so sorry. I didn't even think about what would happen if you got hurt."

"It's okay, Quinn. I agreed to do it knowing my limitations." Dang it, but she looked cute when she was worried, her pretty face all scrunched up like that.

"Well, the next thing I have planned isn't half as dangerous to your championship hopes."

And she was right. Looking at flowers and fancy sculptures inside a casino wasn't dangerous to his body, but he worried every time he turned around that he was liable to bump into something expensive and break it. Maybe it was dangerous after all. Only this time, to his wallet.

Quinn pointed up to the glass ceiling. "They lower in everything through special windows. The whole thing opens up and they lower it down with a crane."

"And they do this every Christmas?" Jackson looked around, appreciating the effort. Fake snow gently cascaded from hidden vaults above them, automated polar bears played with frolicking penguins, and everywhere, there were Christmas scenes that had been made from flowers.

"Well, the Christmas scene is once a year, but they change the main display every couple of months." She peered up at him from beneath sooty, lowered eyelashes. "Do you need to go soon to start getting ready for tonight?" She looked like a little kid who had just had her candy taken away from her.

"Yeah, I do, but I was thinking..." Dang it, if his heart didn't start pounding in his ears. "If you don't have plans tonight, maybe you could come back behind the chutes with me?"

"I'd love to." She bit down on her full bottom lip. "I mean, if you don't think I'll be a distraction or in the way?"

"I think you will be a distraction in the best kind of way. You can be my lucky charm."

"I need to go back to my place first. Will we have time?"

Jackson reached out for her hand. He wasn't going to waste the opportunity to touch her. Heck, he felt proud as punch as they promenaded back the way they'd come, appreciating the woman who was at his side. As they made their way through the casino gaming area, he could feel himself being scrutinized. His gaze sweeping the area, he made out a smaller man in an immaculate suit standing beside another slightly taller version. Their looks didn't exactly give Jackson the warm fuzzies.

Quinn led him to a corridor that was slightly removed from the rest. "It's a private elevator," she explained as she pressed the button.

"Do all of the staff live here, too?" He couldn't imagine that would leave a lot of room for paying guests, given how many workers he'd seen just from their walk.

"No. Actually, Kelly and I are the only ones. With what we do, they wanted us to be easily accessible and not have to travel. Our jobs require us to be flexible in our hours." Jackson was beginning to wonder what he'd stepped into as she opened the door to her and Kelly's suite. He'd never seen anything like it, and the fact that the casino had just given it to them for accommodation … well, Quinn was certainly leading a very different life to the one he was. "I won't be a moment," she said, heading to the kitchen.

Jackson gave a start of surprise as easily the biggest cat he'd ever seen padded out of a room and across the floor in front of him. There was a decidedly matronly wobble to her, one he'd seen in a lot of critters on the ranch in his time. The giant feline was in the family way.

Quinn set down a dish of food in the kitchen and knelt

beside the cat as it began to eat. "This is Duchess. She adopted me a little while ago."

"And you're going to be a grandmother soon by the looks of that belly on her."

"Yeah, can you believe she was someone's pet and they didn't want her and just left her at an animal shelter in this state?" A passion blazed from Quinn's eyes as she railed at the injustice that had been done to her cat. Jackson thought she'd never looked more beautiful.

"I don't understand how people do that either, but it looks like she's landed on her paws with you."

"Yeah." Quinn stood and began to fill up a dish with fresh water. "I just need to go and quickly change her kitty litter tray and then I'm already to go."

"I can do that for you."

Quinn looked horrified. "There's no way I'm letting you clean out the mess from my cat."

"You forget I live on a ranch. At least, when I'm not on the road," he quantified.

"Well then, Mr Tough Cowboy, if her kitty tray ever needs cleaning out on your ranch, you'll be the first to know." The look she threw him was pure sass. Dang, this girl was getting under his skin. "Now, I better hurry up or we'll be late." Somehow, Jackson felt he really ought to care about being late more than he did.

THE FLASHING LASER lights were blinding and then suddenly the main arena was flooded with light. The music began to swell, the crowd twitching with anticipation, and then a cavalcade of riders entered the arena. Looking right at home on horseback, Quinn could see Jackson proudly riding behind the Colorado state flag, his head held high, shoulders thrown back as he waved to the crowd. Judging by the number of women who pressed around the edges of the grandstand hoping to get a closer look at him, Jackson was a favorite with the ladies. Uninvited jealousy flared uncomfortably in Quinn's stomach. She'd never been the jealous type before, and it didn't sit well with her that she should start to experience it now. And over what? Some women waving signs and blowing kisses at a man she'd really only known for days. *You need to get a grip, girl.* She found herself hoping he would look in her direction.

Quinn flattered herself as she imagined him scanning the crowds near where she stood behind the rails, looking for her. After a final lap, the parade of horseback-mounted competitors exited the arena to much cheering and hollering.

She made her way to the spot Jackson had told her to meet him at and settled in to watch the parade of personalities come by as she waited. Quinn chuckled to herself at the memory that she'd felt out of place at the rodeo she'd attended back in Australia, but boy, oh boy, this was next level. The women who walked by—and she could only assume they were partners and wives of some of the competitors—were decked out in tasseled, sequined numbers that looked like they'd stepped out of a western magazine. Quinn was secretly envious that they could pull of the looks and pondered what her chances were of doing the same. She was still mulling over the possibility when a shadow fell over her.

"I like the idea of coming back here to you." Jackson's deep voice wrapped around her like the softest of blankets, leaving her bathed in warmth.

"I like the idea of waiting here for you." Quinn wanted to kick herself once the words were out of her mouth. In her mind, they hadn't sounded so cheesy and, well, like some sort of waiting doormat. "You looked good out there."

"It's funny, before we go out, I hate it. My palms start sweating and I feel sick to my stomach. And then I get out there and I enjoy it every dang time." He reached into his pocket and pulled a lanyard out, draping it over her neck. "Now, this means you can officially come back with me and hang out behind the chutes." He held his hand out to her.

Gladly, she slipped hers snuggly into his warm, firm grip and walked beside him, glancing around as they went. Some paramedic-type people appeared to be setting up in a series of rooms near the cavernous space beneath the grandstands. Looking at their signage, it appeared they were sponsored by a major western wear company. Further along, she could see cowboys in various stages of undress, most heavily strapped up as they began to prepare for the contest against beast that was in store for them. It made Quinn think of how gladiators might have prepared below the Colosseum, hearing the roars of the crowd above baying for blood. A shiver danced up her spine, making her clutch Jackson's hand tighter.

He looked down, his brow raised in askance at the sudden pressure. Quinn shook her head dismissively, a light smile on her lips. At last, he brought her to a room where a vaguely familiar blonde woman sat with twin toddlers. Recognition flared to life in her. It was Frankie, Luciano's wife, and their children.

"Quinn, I need to go and get ready, I'll come back before I head up to the chutes and we can find a place for you to stand and watch my ride."

"She'll be fine here with me," Frankie said, giving Quinn a friendly smile. "I'll make sure we don't get up to too much mischief."

There was something about the other woman's easy friendliness that made Quinn feel right at home, no matter how different their outwardly appearances. "I'm sure Frankie and I will be fine. Us Aussies have to stick together."

"I promise I won't be long." Jackson looked like he wanted to say more, his mouth worked like he was on the verge of saying something but, at the last minute, he obviously changed his mind. He touched his fingers to the brim of his hat and walked away. Quinn was confused to what had just transpired.

"You'll get used to it," Frankie said. Quinn looked at her in surprise. Did she have some sort of insight into what Jackson was going to say? Her hopes for enlightenment was dashed at the blonde woman's next words. "Your man leaving you to prepare, the waiting around, the fear that they won't come back." There was a strength to Frankie's easy acceptance.

"Oh, Jackson isn't my man. I mean, we've only really just met again."

Frankie had the good manners to stifle the disbelief that flittered across her face. "I see."

"But how do you manage with all of this? You and Luciano have been together for a while." Quinn gestured to the twins as proof.

The other woman's face softened as she looked down at her children locked in a ferocious game of one building blocks for the other to knock it down. "I never spent my time waiting around. It has only been the last few years that I've come to some of his events. Obviously, a fair few of them before that, I was competing myself." A lingering trace of fire flickered to life in her eyes, a hint of the champion she must have been.

"I'm sorry, I didn't know you competed. I don't really know much about rodeos." She glanced down at her outfit, still feeling out of place. "Not that you could tell."

Frankie laughed lightly at her candor. "You hide it well."

Quinn found that she liked her fellow countrywoman immensely as they sat chatting and talking about back home. She was taken by surprise when Jackson reappeared, now dressed in wide-legged leather chaps. There was a distinctive swishing as he walked toward her, and his wrist was strapped and a protection vest hung open.

"Are you ready?" he asked.

She stopped her obvious appraisal of him, feeling herself grow hotter as he caught her gawking at him. "I guess the question should be are you ready?"

That smile, the one that said he knew exactly how it affected the other person but he was still somewhat embarrassed by the impact it had on others, beamed out at her, those blue eyes put to devastating effect. Quinn felt her knees weaken under the onslaught of the man's sheer magnetism.

"I'm always ready." Quinn wasn't sure if he was still talking about bull riding or something else. And frankly, she didn't care.

The next moments went by in a blur as she was still caught up in the vortex of what, affection? No, affection was too insipid a word. Longing? Yearning? Whatever it was, it felt rich, multilayered, and something she hoped to never stop feeling. When she finally came back to some resemblance of normalcy, she was wedged on the rails behind the chute, a clear view to a bull below and out into the arena. She was surrounded by cowboys in their leather, denim and hats. Here at the rail, the smell of livestock was strong, the scent of masculine anticipation thick. Jackson forced his way to her side, and she turned to face him. He gently raised her chin with his hand, his expression fierce with excitement and something else she couldn't quite decipher.

"Wish me luck."

"I wish you luck with every fiber of my being." *Where on earth were all these cheesy lines coming from? She sounded like something out of a bad romance novel.*

Those piercing sky-blue eyes bored into her for a

moment longer, and then he nodded to a man beside her. He let go of her chin and zipped up his vest. "I won't be long."

Jackson swung himself up onto the rail and began to lower himself down. After that, it all happened so fast. The bull leaping away. The cowboys on each side of Quinn pressing forward, leaning over the rails and partially blocking her view. The same cowboys, yipping and hollering. Quinn could only make out flashes of him, and then a buzzer went and the bull riders around her roared their approval, the sound echoing back from the crowd in the stands.

She might not know rodeo, but she did know how to read the situation in that moment. Jackson had done well and, more than that, apparently he wasn't hurt either. It was only as that realization struck her that she became aware of her tight grip on the cold metal, her knuckles having long ago turned white from the pressure. She forced herself to let go as Jackson made his way back to her, triumph stamped on every grain of his being. Quinn's mouth went dry at the sight, her heart pounding as she waited for him, his progress slower than she would have liked as he was congratulated by his fellow bull riders on the way.

"I told you I was ready."

She was still thinking about that moment later that evening as he escorted her back to The Chimera—and what an evening it had been. Jackson had been crowned that night's go round champion and received a buckle. That experience had been up there with one of the most surreal moments of her life. She'd accompanied him to another venue, and there with the rest of that night's winners had, one at a time, gone out onto a stage for their presentation in front of a packed room of boisterous fans. To add to the moment, Jackson had insisted on her joining him up there. For a humble Colorado cowboy, he certainly had a knack for giving her experiences that no one else ever had. Now that they were about to enter The Chimera, Quinn realized she wasn't ready for the night to end.

"Jackson, do you mind if we take a quick detour? There's one more thing I'd like to show you. It won't take long."

"Of course."

"It's just over there." Quinn pointed to a casino across the road. Strains of Christmas carols floated on the wind to them, the slightest of whispers over the noise of revelers and traffic.

Jackson's brow furrowed as he caught the tune, a lopsided smile appearing as it registered. "Are we going to do one more Christmas thing this evening?"

"You betcha." She led the way until they were standing in front of an expanse of water, the surface like a sheet of glass reflecting the lights of the skyscrapers above them. Crowds were already beginning to gather. Suddenly, ripples began to appear, distorting the images as water jets began to protrude out in readiness. "You've probably seen the famous fountains before, but hopefully never like this."

Jackson leaned forward. Even in the dim light, she could see a gleam of anticipation. And then, at precisely the same time as *Jingle Bell Rock* split through the night sky, the first sprays of water shot up, seemingly determined to reach the very moon.

"I'm beginning to think Vegas does Christmas unlike anywhere else," Jackson said, not taking his eyes off the spectacle. Quinn found herself splitting her attention between the choreography of the fountains in front of her and the cowboy who watched enthralled.

As the last strains of the song came to a close, he turned toward her. In the dim lighting, his eyes were no longer the bright blue of tropical Tahitian waters. Instead, they'd turned to inky pools. Quinn was drowning in them, seeing her own emotions staring back at her, feelings that were too soon for either of them to be experiencing. He gently reached out and tucked a stray piece of hair behind her ear, the gesture one of infinite tenderness.

Quinn could barely breathe, her lungs sucked free of all oxygen. Energy rippled through their locked gazes and, for the longest of moments, neither of them moved, time stretching out between them. Slowly, he began to lower his head. When their lips were only a whisper apart, she could feel her whole body trembling, and as his lips finally met hers, she found herself melting from his kiss. He pulled back with a tender smile and Quinn breathed deeply of the cool night air—anything to slow the beating tattoo of her heart.

It was beginning to feel a lot like Christmas, after all.

CHAPTER 14

*D*ang, *he was starting to feel like an old man,* Jackson thought as his joints let out muffled pops and creaks as he stretched his lanky frame. Kissing Quinn in front of the fountains the night before with Christmas carols floating on the breeze around them, it was a moment that seemed like a dream. She was everything he'd ever wanted, ever wished for. He'd suspected it before now, but the more he spent time with her, the more he was certain deep in his soul that she was the one his heart called out for.

Energized at the thought of his beautiful Australian girl, he threw the covers back and sprung from bed, a move that he instantly regretted as his body reminded him that he'd spent part of the previous evening tangoing with a rightly annoyed bull. Much more cautiously, he padded over to the bathroom, turned the faucet on, and waited as the water ran hot. Stepping in, he let the warm liquid cascade over his body, working its magic into tired and sore muscles. Resting his head against the cool of the tiles, he breathed in deeply of the steamy air.

"Quinn," he slowly exhaled her name. Abruptly, his stomach gave a lurch. After today, she was back to work. Pragmatically, his head understood that Quinn was an independent woman who had commitments other than himself, but his heart railed against the injustice of not being able to spend time with her. *Well, I just need to make the time I have with her count.*

Determinedly, he turned off the water and began to towel himself off. He wasn't going to waste a single moment. Picking up his phone, he dialed Quinn's number. Hearing her voice, husky from sleep, he knew he was lost. And honestly, he didn't mind at all. "I didn't mean to wake you up."

He could hear the bed covers rustling and pictured her smiling. "No, I took a while to fall asleep last night. I kept thinking about that kiss."

"Thinking about it in a good way or a bad way?" Jackson's vanity couldn't resist asking.

A light tinkle of laughter greeted his question. "In a good way. A very good way."

His masculine pride swelled up at her words. "I was wondering what you had planned for today?"

"Um, I was supposed to have today off, but Kelly has had a bit of a situation and needs my help. But I'll be free tonight."

"Care to hang out with me while I compete? I mean, if you don't, I can swing by afterwards and we can do something then." Jackson waited with bated breath, surprising himself with how nervous he felt for her answer.

"Don't be silly. I loved watching you last night. Do you want me to meet you there?"

"No, I'll pick you up."

"Jackson?" her voice was soft.

"Yeah?"

"I can't wait to see you again."

His heart began to thud. "Me neither." He hung up the phone, staring at it for a moment before leaping up and energetically punching the air like he'd just scored a touchdown. Perhaps he had.

By the time evening came, Jackson didn't think he would ever get tired of looking at Quinn. Every time he saw her, there was some nuance—a new discovery. Tonight, it was the fact that one of her front teeth was ever so slightly crooked. It was so minute that he figured a person would only notice if they had the pleasure of being in her company for a while. He thought it was cute, but knowing the pride that she took in her appearance, he bet Quinn hated it. Once again with his lucky charm by his side, he'd ridden the best ride of his career. There was something about having her there that lifted him, made him more than he was. When he'd walked onto the stage at the afterparty to receive his go round winner's buckle for the second night in a row with her by his side, well, he'd thought he was just about to explode with pride.

He smiled down at her as she pointed excitedly to another Christmas window decoration. After a bite to eat, it had been her suggestion to take a stroll down the promenade to see the decorations and carolers. Her eyes sparkled up at him in excitement as she clapped her hands together. "Did you see the gingerbread house? How on earth did they make one so big?"

"I want to know where they got all the supersized candy from." He pulled her close and planted a kiss on the top of her head.

"Oh, that's easy. At the famous Candy Station stores we have here on The Strip. When Kelly and I first went in there, they had a gob stopper that was bigger than my fist." She held up her clenched hand to emphasis her point.

"The Christmas windows are a lot different in Colorado," he said as they continued their walk, taking in the sights. "Actually, a lot of the Christmas stuff is different."

Her face scrunched up adorably. "How so?"

"Well, it's the same types of things, I guess, just a different way of doing them. The window decorations here sure are fancy, but I don't know. They seem too bright, too fancy. The ones back home, the store owners fix them up with fir branches and have little scenes that are, I don't know, homey."

"I think I get what you're saying."

"We have ice skating too, but it's in a pond and there are pines around it. The snow is real, too."

Quinn cocked her head to one side, contemplating his words. "It has that quality that makes it feel like Christmas to you. I guess it's what you're used to. Christmas here is like how everything on The Strip is. Loud, bright and over the top."

Jackson stepped around a panhandler who was dressed as a showgirl, her outfit red and white with strategically placed pieces of white fur. "Oh, it's definitely over the top. I guess I should be getting you back home." Regret laced his words. After tonight, he wasn't sure when he'd be able to see her again.

"I wish you didn't, but I need to get some sleep before my high roller arrives. He's demanding at the best of times, but with hardly any sleep, he's going to be bloody taxing."

He didn't like the thought of her being at another man's beck and call, but she did have a job to do. Slowly, they turned around and made their way back the way they'd come from. Jackson found his steps getting slower, trying to draw out the inevitable.

"Jackson?"

"Yes?"

"I want you to promise me that you'll get someone to video your rides so you can send them through to me." Quinn earnestly stared up at him as they came to a stop in front of The Chimera.

"I promise."

"And I expect you to keep winning, too."

He felt his lips quirk. "Yes, ma'am."

She put her hands on her hips. "I mean it, mister."

"I promise. Or would you feel better if we sealed it with a kiss?"

Her gorgeous full lips stretched into an inviting smile. "I think it would be for the best. Just to make sure you take your promise seriously."

"Of course." The words were whispered against her mouth as he pulled her into his arms and began to kiss her soundly.

~

QUINN HAD BEEN WRAPPED up in a warm glow of happiness since she'd woken up that morning. It seemed that in the days since Jackson had reappeared, there was quite simply no other mood to be in.

"I knew you would be happy to see me."

The smile slipped right off her face. Apparently, she was wrong. "Hello, Markus. I trust your flight was good."

"Tolerable. I will be going to the tables immediately." She could feel his eyes roam over her body, even though they were shielded by his sunglasses. Quinn tried to arrange her features into a semblance of polite professionalism rather than the distaste that coursed through her. "I want dinner arranged in my suite for two at nine pm. When you're finished with that, you will join me in the high stakes room."

Without sparing a further glance in her direction, he strode off, leaving Quinn glaring at his departing back.

Give me strength. Drawing on a deep well of internal fortitude she didn't know she possessed, she walked over to Julie's desk. "Mr Jamison would like dinner for two in his suite this evening."

Julie gave her a sympathetic smile. "Did he have any particular request?"

"None, but make sure there is plenty of Cristal in his room and an extra bottle of his favorite Tequila. When they set the room up, dress it with extra candles. I gather he plans to be entertaining someone special tonight."

"Lucky you. You might even get to go see your cowboy if that's the case." Julie gave her a knowing look.

Hope sparked to life inside Quinn. She hadn't even thought about the possibility of seeing Jackson when Markus had been ordering her around. "That would just be the best. I'd better head up to the high stakes room. I've been informed that my presence is required."

The afternoon and evening went surprisingly quickly, Quinn allowing her mind to drift to happy thoughts that centered around Jackson and kisses set against a Christmas-themed backdrop. In fact, she was so caught up that Markus had to tap her arm three times before she came back to reality with a thud.

"Thanks for joining us," he sneered at her.

"I'm sorry, I was practicing meditation. I read somewhere recently that it can help in torturous situations." She smiled sweetly at him. "What were you saying?"

"I was saying that you need to go up and start getting ready." Quinn glanced at her watch. It was nearly eight thirty in the evening, which would give her time to spend a few hours with Jackson before she'd have to call it a night. She was dying to know how he'd done. Confusion suddenly rained down on her. How did Markus know that she wanted to meet up with Jackson?

"I'm sorry, get ready for what?"

"I love how she plays dumb when she knows perfectly well what I'm talking about," Markus said condescendingly to his fellow gamblers gathered around the table. "I want you to get ready for dinner with me tonight. The one I asked you to organize."

Cold flooded Quinn's body, dousing the happy glow she'd nurtured all evening. Horrified, she looked at Markus as she grasped what he was saying. He hadn't meant to spend the evening with someone else, thus freeing her up to see Jackson. He'd meant for her to spend it with him.

"There's a lovely dancer who's currently performing as part of the show here. If you like, I can arrange for her to be your dinner companion." Quinn desperately hoped the offer sounded attractive to Markus.

His eyes went flat and unfriendly, his mouth a thin slash on his face. This was not a man who enjoyed being disobeyed. "I think I've made my request quite plain. If you're having difficulties understanding them, I'm sure Lachlan would be more than capable of explaining it to you."

Breathe, Quinn. That's it. Nice, deep breaths, in and out. "If you gentlemen will excuse me"—she smiled graciously at the rest of the assembled company—"it appears that I need to go freshen up." Head held high, she strode from the room before she said something she knew she would regret.

At last gaining the sanctuary of her suite, she picked up the nearest cushion off the sofa and hurled it against the window, unleashing an unladylike string of profanities that fairly turned the air blue. Duchess, from where she reclined awkwardly with her belly pushed out, opened an eye, surveyed the situation, and finding it beneath her, closed it again.

Still overflowing with rage and her chest heaving, Quinn clenched her hands at her side. Frustrated tears burned her eyes. She hated how Markus talked to her. Most of the other high rollers she could handle—some were even nice—but every time he was there, he eroded her worth. The thought that she would now have to spend more of the evening with him and the loss of how she'd thought she'd be able to spend it with Jackson made a sob escape her. She was beginning to hate this city.

Feeling helpless now that her anger had been spent, Quinn sat down beside Duchess, who let out a low purr, the only sign that she acknowledged her presence. "I hate this, Duchess." She scrubbed at her eyes, dashing the tears away. "I just need to figure out what I'm going to do about it." Feeling a determination that was at odds with any semblance of a plan, she stood. If Markus wanted dinner with her, then that's what he was going to get. It just might not be the one he had in mind.

Markus's left eye twitched as he took in her appearance. It had taken a while for inspiration to strike when Quinn had been getting ready, but when it had, she'd fully committed to it. "I thought I asked you to get ready for dinner?" he asked.

She innocently looked down at her baggy, discolored sweatpants, oversized T-shirt and Ugg boots—an outfit that was normally solely reserved for the privacy of home. "I assumed that, since it was just an informal dinner in your suite, I could wear something comfortable." She patted him on the cheek as she pushed past him into the room. "I know you have my wellbeing first and foremost in your mind."

Quinn heard the door click as he shut it behind her. "Of course. I believe dinner will be arriving shortly. Would you care for a glass of champagne?"

"Thank you, that would be lovely." She waited as he opened the bottle, jumping at the loud pop. "I meant what I said earlier. Jess is a lovely girl and would be quite eager to keep you company." She accepted the glass and took a sip, the bubbles tickling her nose.

Markus sent her an annoyed glare, his nostrils flaring. "I think you know me well enough to know that, if I want the undoubtedly lovely Jess here, I would have requested it." He looked at her over the rim of his glass as he sipped his own champagne, a canny intelligence piercing her. "You and I both know that you'll only keep this charade up for so long." He raised his index finger, pointing at her. "Granted, I enjoy the chase as much as the next man, sometimes even more. But in the end, we both know how this story ends."

"Where the feisty chick tells the overbearing jerk of a whale that she's a professional doing her job and that in no way grants him the right to anything more?" Quinn struggled to get the words out, her mounting fury choking her.

"If that's how you want to play this." Markus smirked at her, raising his glass in salute.

"I'm not playing anything. I'm going to put all my cards on the table so you can see for yourself what hand I'm actually holding. I don't like you. I think you're a horrible human being, and I dread every time I find out that you're coming to The Chimera and I'll be forced to be in your company again. And my telling you that I'm not interested, never have been, never will be, should be enough. You should respect that and leave me alone except for in a professional capacity. But clearly, it isn't. So let me help get you over the line. I'm seeing someone else, and it's serious."

"Get rid of him." Markus's eyes were flinty as he glared at her, stepping forcefully into her personal space.

Quinn had no doubts he was trying to intimidate her. She drew herself up to her full height and thrust her chin out. "Not going to happen. And you can run to Lachlan all you want, but I'm never getting rid of him."

A vein bulged in Markus's neck, a muscle twitching in his jaw. It was the first time Quinn had seen an emotion in him that wasn't tightly controlled, and despite her bravado, it was terrifying. His eyes narrowed menacingly as he continued to glare at her, hostility radiating off him and then, like a curtain coming down, he smirked at her.

"Don't try to bluff a man who's as good at gambling as I am. I'll take your wager and raise it. By Christmas, you'll not only have gotten rid of him, but you'll be spending it with me."

Quinn's jaw dropped open at the head-spinning change of direction and shock at the man's sheer audacity. "It's going to be a very cold day in you-know-where before that happens."

"I like those odds. Now, would you like more champagne?" Markus held up the bottle.

"I have a headache, and I think it's best for my health if I leave. I'm sure Lachlan will understand since I haven't taken sick leave since I started." Quinn didn't even bother waiting for whatever rude nonsense was going to come out of his mouth next, simply heading for the door.

"Quinn, remember to pack warm. You're going to love St Moritz at Christmastime."

She closed the door firmly on his parting remark. Disappointment washed over her. Knowing there was a very high probability of Markus already being on the phone to Lachlan, it meant it was impossible for her to slip out and catch up with

Jackson. A warm glow chased away the dejection, but she could still do the next best thing—snuggle in bed and talk to her gorgeous Colorado cowboy on the phone until she fell asleep to his dulcet tones. With the spring restored to her step, she headed home, proud for having stood up for herself, even if there was going to be one heck of a price to pay for it in the morning.

CHAPTER 15

Jackson stared at the phone, amazed at the changes a simple conversation with Quinn had wrought over him. The bitter disappointment he'd felt at not riding to his own exacting standard had made him return to his room to wallow in frustration. And then, like an angel, she'd known. Just like that, she'd tamed the beast that had raged inside of him, quietening it with her soothing tones. He wasn't sure how he was going to manage in two days when it would all be over and he'd be heading home. Jackson glanced at his watch, knowing that his mom was probably waiting up for him to check in with her and let her know how he'd gone.

He smiled as he thought of her sitting in front of the television, a fire roaring in the fireplace as she sat beside his father, a blanket over both their knees as she watched her favorite program and Dad pretended to complain but secretly enjoyed them. Jackson started to dial.

"Hello. How'd you go tonight, son?" Jackson could hear the television in the background.

"Not as good tonight, Mom."

"Did you get hurt?"

"No."

"Then it sounds like it was an all right night to me." Jackson had to give it to her, she was right. Anytime you sat on a bull and got to walk away from it unhurt was a good night. "Where did you end up placing?"

"I came third."

"Well, buck up, boy. I didn't raise you to be a bad loser. Third place is still something to be proud of."

"I know. It's not that." It was true. He knew in his heart that he was coming to the end of his career and he wanted to make each ride count, like it might be the last time he entered the arena. Tonight, not having Quinn there, everything had felt off.

"Then what is it?"

"There's this girl," he began, not sure if he could put into words what she meant to him. He was pretty sure he could spend a lifetime searching for the words and still not find them.

"And does this girl have a name?"

"Quinn."

"That's a lovely name. Was Quinn there tonight? Is that why you're feeling down? Because you wanted to impress her?"

"She wasn't there tonight, she had to work. But she's been there the nights that I've won. I guess, maybe, she was my lucky charm. I don't know, Mom. She's gotten under my skin. I spend an awful lot of time thinking about her."

He could almost hear the smile in his mother's voice when she replied. "About time a girl got under your skin. Your pa and I were beginning to think it was never going to happen. Well, tell me all about her."

Jackson didn't need any more encouragement. "She beautiful, Mom, and smart. She's actually Australian. I met her when I was down under last year and somehow we met up again here this year."

"Sounds like it's fate that you two met up again. Does she live in Vegas now?"

"Yeah, she works at one of the big fancy casinos here and she even lives there with her friend in a suite high above The Strip, looking down on it."

"She must have an important job if they put her up in an expensive room like that."

"She does. She had to work tonight, otherwise she'd have been there to see me ride. Actually, she's going to miss the last day of the NFR."

"And then you'll be leaving to come home for Christmas." His mother's voice was sympathetic on the other end of the line. Jackson's stomach twisted at the thought of leaving Quinn.

"Yeah."

"Well, have you asked her what her plans are for Christmas? Why don't you ask her if she wants to come here?"

Jackson felt like his mother had just slapped him in the face. What a rookie mistake. It was so obvious, and yet had somehow eluded him while he wallowed in self-induced misery. "I never actually thought of it," he admitted. "But it seems like too good of an idea to waste. If she says yes, better make room at the table for another person. I'll be bringing her home for Christmas."

THERE WAS a bounce to Quinn's step as she ushered Markus across the polished marble foyer that reflected the jubilance that frothed and bubbled inside her. As soon as she got him safely ensconced on his private jet, winging off to destinations unknown, she would be free to see Jackson one last time before he left. Her stomach knotted painfully at the thought of him leaving and not knowing when she would see him again. She was devastated that she'd had to miss his last ride of the NFR and being there to celebrate his runner up buckle. Markus might have let her mini revolt slide by without a complaint to Lachlan, but that didn't mean she was off the hook. In fact, her defiance had proven to solidify his determination that she must succumb to his charms.

Now, locking on to the limo that would take them to the airport, she pushed away her exhaustion at fending off his advances and the ache in her heart from missing Jackson.

"Slow down, I'm in no rush. That's one of the perks of having a private plane." Quinn wanted to roll her eyes at his smarmy voice. "I have something for you." He reached into the inside pocket of his jacket and pulled out a velvet jewelry box.

"I appreciate the gesture, but unfortunately, I can't accept it."

"That didn't stop you from accepting my last gift." Markus thrust the box at her. Quinn put her hands behind her back, out of reach.

"I am often given gifts as a show of appreciation for my service in this role, and that is the spirit in which I accepted your prior gift. Given that you're now seeking to change the nature of our professional relationship into something else, I believe that it would be inappropriate for me to accept." It gave her a small sense of satisfaction to see his eyes narrow at her rebuttal. From the corner of her eye, she caught sight of Jackson standing awkwardly, watching the exchange. She smiled politely at Markus. "If you'll excuse me for a moment, there's something I need to take care of. I'll meet you in the limo." He opened his mouth to argue, but she was already walking away from him.

Quinn could feel her soul lighten as she almost skipped

her way to Jackson and gave him a quick hug. "I'm so glad to see you. You have no idea how much I've missed you."

His smile seemed a bit forced as he returned hers. "I was going to call, but I decided to take a chance on you being free to talk."

Quinn's stomach clenched at having to let him down. "I have to take Markus to the airport and then make sure he gets on the plane. I don't want to take any chances of him bloody hanging around longer than he has to." There was a tightness to Jackson's face that concerned her. "We can catch up tonight? I'm free then."

"Sure thing, it wasn't important." He looked over her shoulder, Quinn following his gaze to see Markus still standing where she'd left him. "I'd better let you get back to work."

"I'll see you tonight," Quinn found herself saying to Jackson's departing back. *What on Earth had just happened?* He'd seemed to shut off somehow. Sighing, she made her way back to Markus and escorted him to the limo.

She was still mulling over the change in Jackson as the streetscape flashed past outside her car window. "I'll be back two days before Christmas to collect you," Markus said.

"I have other plans." Quinn didn't care if that meant sitting with Duchess and eating tinned soup together. There was no way she was spending Christmas with him.

"With that country hick cowboy back at the casino? Quinn, a woman like you—you want the life I can give you, not one living on some back-county ranch." His eyes bored into her, his face losing all trace of softness. "Cancel them."

"I don't work for you, and I'm not bloody going to cancel anything."

Markus pressed his shoulders back into the leather of his seat. "We'll see."

Something in the condescending way he said it or the

complete confidence he had that he would bend her to his will gave her flashbacks to twelve months earlier with Lance. The way he wore his wealth like armor, the expensive suits and flashy watches, making people jump to attention at his slightest whim. Maybe it was because, deep down, for all his mocking of Jackson, he knew he didn't hold a candle to the sort of man he was.

She'd take Jackson in his Levi's and slightly scratched-up boots any day of the week.

Later that evening as she watched Jackson lying on the floor and playing gently with Duchess, she didn't think she could conjure up anything sexier than a blue-eyed cowboy lying on the floor in his jeans and sock clad feet.

"Thanks for not minding that we eat in tonight. I haven't had much time to spend with Duchess and I know she's been wanting some attention." When she glanced down, she could see him looking at her with a strange expression on his face. A sliver of worry wormed its way into her happiness.

"I love nothing better than to not have to get fancied up and be able to just relax. I'm happy to simply be here with you." Her heart melted as she felt his gaze like a warm caress, chasing away her concerns of only moments before. "Actually, there's something I want to ask you."

Quinn thought her heart was about to beat out of her chest. "Yes?"

His eyelashes lowered, shielding his eyes from her. "If you don't have plans for Christmas, I was hoping you might want to spend it at the ranch with me—and my family, of course," he hastily added.

"I would love to. I've never had a proper white Christmas before." Her excitement turned to disappointment as she looked down at her heavily pregnant cat. "But I don't want to leave Duchess, and she's due just after Christmas."

He stared straight at her, undaunted, and smiling guilelessly. "Bring her. She won't be the first animal to give birth at the ranch."

Quinn found herself beaming back at him as she burst out in laughter. "I don't imagine she is. Well then, Jackson Gregory, I'd be honored to spend Christmas with you and your family."

COLORADO SPRINGS

*J*ackson stretched his long legs out in front of him, crossing them at the ankles before uncrossing them and folding his arms. He glanced at his watch, giving it a little shake to make sure it was still working. The plastic seat groaned as he pivoted to peer at the arrival's information again. Nothing had changed on that front either. Giving a sniff, he slumped back in his chair and then straightened up again to keep the flowers he held in his hands safely away from his shirt.

He'd wanted to bring something to surprise Quinn, to see that beaming smile that lit up her entire face. The one he missed so much—and he'd only been away from it for a few days. Now he felt stupid for the idea. Watching that highfalutin flatlander giving Quinn a piece of jewelry that was probably worth more than his truck had made him feel about five inches tall. How did a guy who made his living riding bulls compete with that? Heck, he wasn't even going to be doing that soon. Then he'd just be a rancher. Jackson scratched at his neck as he tried to picture Quinn as a rancher's wife. The high heels and fancy clothes she favored weren't exactly made with Colorado ranching life in mind.

Unbidden, an image of her appeared in his mind, her caramel hair flowing down her back, her belly softly swollen as she stood in a simple dress. His baby. Jackson jerked his mind away from that particular direction, for surely that was only going to end in heartbreak. Sure, Quinn might come and play rancher girlfriend for a week or two, but there was no way she'd want this forever.

He ran a finger inside his collar, pulling it slightly away from his neck. The stale airport air felt stuffy, and his hands were sweaty against the plastic covering the stems of the bouquet. Uniformed airline staff bustled past him, the smell of perfume, hairspray and breath mints lingering in their wake. The incessant generic Christmas carols that had been playing over the loudspeaker cut out.

"Ladies and gentlemen, flight D294 from Las Vegas has just landed. Arrivals will be through gate 28."

Jackson double-checked the large white numbering above the glass door where staff that had only moments before breezed past him were now busily preparing for an influx of humanity. The beating of his heart began to steadily build as people filtered out. His eyes scanned the crowd, flitting past joyous greetings and loud complaints of the trials of air travel and skimmed over ugly Christmas sweaters and squealing children. And then he saw her. It was like a scene from a movie—the ones where everything is in black and white until a woman walks into the room, bringing a spark of color that starts with her and then radiates out to encompass the entire setting in glorious technicolor.

Quinn stood in her thigh-high leather boots, black leggings and oversized sweater, her ever-present handbag hanging from her arm as she anxiously scanned the room. And then across the crowd, their eyes met, and her entire face glowed, beaming a joyous smile of recognition. Jackson felt his face stretch into a goofy grin in reply. Seeing her again, it was like seeing her for the first time all over again. The way she looked at him as she ran over fairly knocked the air from his lungs. Would he ever get used to seeing her and how she made him feel? No, he never wanted to take this feeling for granted.

And then she was in his arms, and he was picking her up, her feet dangling to the ground, her arms entwined around his neck. *Dang, she smelled good. Like gardenias and roses. Heck, even her hair smelled of flowers.* And then her lips were hot and sweet against his as he lost himself to anything but the softness of their kiss and the delicate floral fragrance of her perfume. Something about flowers tickled at the edge of his psyche. With a start, he almost dropped Quinn in his haste to return her to the ground.

Her mouth formed a perfect 'O' of surprise at her sudden drop in altitude. "I got these for you." Jackson held out the previously forgotten flowers, now looking a little worse for wear after his rather enthusiastic greeting. Sheepishly, he handed them over.

Quinn looked like she'd just received the crown jewels. She held them to her nose and breathed in their fragrance deeply. "They're beautiful." Her gorgeous hazel-green eyes glowed like rare and exotic gems as she looked up at him.

Jackson looked doubtfully down, noting the broken stems and drooping petals. "I'm not so sure about that."

She gave him a look of reproach. "Something doesn't have to be perfect to still be lovely. I'm sure when I pop them into some water, they'll come good."

Jackson shook his head in wonder at her sentiment. "Well, if you're sure. Did you have a good flight?"

"It was quick, the people around me had good personal hygiene, and I had a fabulous conversation with a great-grandmother from Tanzania on her way to visit her first ever great-grandson. So, yeah, it was good. Better for being here with you now." Her hand crept into his as she spoke.

Jackson felt a surge of warmth from her touch, an awareness that felt like coming home. "I guess we'd better go and collect Duchess and your luggage."

"I hope she traveled okay. The vet gave her a check before we left and said she would be fine for the quick flight." Quinn's brows furrowed, and it took a considerable amount of willpower for Jackson to pull his gaze away from where it was riveted to the sight of her pearly white teeth worrying her bottom lip.

"Well then, we'd best collect her and get her to the comforts of the ranch." With her hand still snuggly secured in his own, they made their way together in search of one pregnant feline and some luggage. Jackson didn't think he'd ever felt happier.

THE TRUCK HAD the faint smell of leather, earth and hay and was exactly what Quinn had envisaged Jackson driving. It was big, solid and dependable-looking and she felt warm and safe as they pulled out of the carpark in the wintery conditions. "Oh my gosh, snow," she squealed, clapping her hands together.

As the plane had been coming into Colorado Springs, the city had unfolded beneath her searching gaze. The city nestled in the foothills of the majestic Rocky Mountains, the snow-capped peaks soaring as if they were striving to reach Heaven itself. Having come from a country where snow was a rarity except for a few select places in winter, she was filled with an almost childish delight at the sheer amount of the white stuff piled up on the edge of the road, yards, roofs and, well, basically everywhere. The shop windows all had Christmas displays, their twinkling lights changing the snow different colors.

"Look, Duchess." She held up the pet carrier so the feline could get a better view. Duchess gave a little mew, but Quinn couldn't be sure if it was a complaint or exclamation of interest.

Jackson gave an indulgent chuckle at her over-the-top reaction. "You won't love it so much when you have to shovel your drive all the time or feed stock up in it."

Quinn poked her tongue out at him. "Party pooper. So, tell me about your ranch. Is it just your mom and dad who live there?" Embarrassed heat crept up from her neck as she guiltily realized she'd never actually asked all that much about the ranch that obviously meant so much to Jackson. *He must think I'm a completely self-absorbed airhead.*

"It's actually my pop and grandma's ranch, and yep, my dad and mom also live there. So does my sister, Beth, and her husband, Levi, and their kids, Jimmy and Laura."

Quinn felt her jaw drop open in shock and she darted a quick look to Jackson, just to be sure he wasn't making fun of her. She vaguely remembered him mentioning something when they'd first met, but it had completely slipped her mind. She swallowed, her mouth suddenly dry at the prospect of meeting his entire family. Somehow, she'd been under the impression that she would only be meeting his parents on this trip. Nervously, she licked her lips.

"Um, and they all live in the same house?"

Jackson laughed, his blue eyes dancing with merriment as they looked at her, the cutest crinkles forming at the corners of them. "Back in the day when Dad and Mom first got married, they lived with Pop and Grandma, but Mom had Dad built a house of their own pretty fast. My uncle, who was a bachelor, passed away a few years back, and Levi and

Beth took over his place on the ranch and extended it to fit the kids in once they came along."

A crazy amount of relief swamped her, and she pursed her lips thoughtfully. Jackson had told her where everyone lived except for one very important family member. "So, where do you live?"

Jackson coughed uncomfortably, shifting his weight in his seat. One hand crept away from the steering wheel to rub the back of his reddening neck. *Well, that's an interesting reaction to a fairly straightforward question.* "I live with my parents. I think I mentioned something about all of this when we first met?"

"Oh." Quinn searched her memory, coming up with only a blank. A lot had happened since then. "It sounds kinda familiar?" she hedged.

"I mean, I'm always on the road, and it doesn't really make much sense for me to have a place of my own right now."

Quinn could feel her eyebrows starting to creep up. Was he planning on making her sleep on the couch? "Where will I be staying?"

Earnest blue eyes met hers, startled at the question. One, apparently, he hadn't been anticipating. "You'll be staying with my dad and mom, too. In my sister's old room, to be exact."

"Okay. You had me bloody worried there for a bit."

The laughter returned to his eyes. "Did you think I was going to make you sleep on the couch?"

"Of course not," denied Quinn. "Well, maybe a little bit."

"I would never do that to you. And I would definitely never do that to Duchess." From the pet carrier, the cat purred her agreement. "You know, I'm going to build a house of my own, one my kids can grow up in. When the snow clears, I'm going to start." His eyes locked on hers with an intensity she couldn't escape, although she hoped he would return his attention to the road before they crashed. "I've been waiting to meet the right woman."

The unspoken question hung between them, and the look he gave her made her belly flip flop. Round and round her head, the question swirled. *Does that mean he thought he'd found her?* Her heart fluttered as delicately as a butterfly with the certainty that he had.

THE RUTTED DRIVE was slushy and slick with snow. *If we ever get a break in the weather, I'm going to have to scrape it with the tractor.* As the truck rattled and swayed, Jackson risked a peek over at Quinn, knowing that, very soon, she would be able to see the compound of houses and farm sheds. He was painfully aware that this wasn't the bright lights and excitement of The Strip like she was used to.

Jackson wondered what it looked like to her—the muddy drive, fields covered with a topping of snow, the gateways churned up from livestock milling. The three shingled houses were all within walking distance to each other. His grandparent's house had a white picket fence out the front. In springtime, roses bloomed behind it, but now it looked barren and bereft of color. The two red barns stood behind the houses—the smaller one could do with a lick of paint, patches peeling off in great flakes.

He squared his shoulders. It might not be polished and shiny like the fancy-pants Chimera, but still it gave him the warm fuzzies that only home could. He watched her face carefully, trying to gauge her reaction as they pulled up.

"Well, here we are." Jackson was at a loss to come up with anything else to say.

Wide, shiny eyes turned toward him. "I've never seen a

place like this in my entire life." *Was that a good thing or a bad thing?* He couldn't be sure. "Jackson, I love it."

The tight knot in his chest loosened as bracing icy air spilled into the cozy interior of the cab when he opened the door, his boots crunching into the snow as he collected her luggage. Quinn followed his lead, clutching the pet carrier in front of her like a shield. *She looks adorable and nervous.* He took her cold hand in his, smiling reassuringly at her as he led her forward onto the porch. Christmas tree lights twinkled through the window, a welcoming glow spilling out. It was like looking into a scene from a book, the window framing the setting perfectly. It shouldn't have surprised him that his entire family was gathered inside, innocently arranged in front of the crackling fire and playing a board game. Jackson knew that they were eagerly waiting to pounce as soon as he and Quinn set foot inside. He glanced down at her from the corner of his eye, considering if it was too late to pack her back into his truck and escape to a nice romantic Bed and Breakfast somewhere in town.

"I should warn you. I think you're about to meet the entire Gregory clan."

She looked up at him from beneath sooty eyelashes, biting her bottom lip, her eyes worried. His attention snagged on the sight of her white teeth pressing against the lush pink. Despite the snow-chilled evening, he began to feel decidedly warm. A blast of toasty air warned Jackson, causing his head to snap around, but not before the mouth that tantalized him stretched into a friendly smile.

So it begins.

"HELLO, Quinn. I'm Hannah, Jackson's mom." His mother stood on the threshold of the house, holding the door open.

Quinn stepped forward, her hand extended in greeting. "Hi, Hannah. I'm Quinn"—she smiled down at the pet carrier —"and this is Duchess."

A black and white border collie came running up, sniffing at the container curiously, tail wagging. Jackson laughingly pushed the dog away. "This is Nitro."

"Well, since Jackson seems bound and determined to keep you both out here in the cold, it looks like it's up to me to get you inside into the warmth." Quickly, Jackson's mom ushered them into the snug house.

"I'm Mike, Jackson's dad." An older, slightly silvered, more lined version of Jackson offered his hand.

Quinn snuck a peek at Jackson, appreciating that he was going to age well. "Hello, Mike. I'm Quinn." She glanced to include Hannah. "Thank you for having me for Christmas."

"You're welcome, sweetheart. Now scoot on in and get a place in front of the fire, I'll bring in a cup of cocoa for you." Hannah made a shooing gesture with her hands.

So far, so good. Quinn's nerves still jangled on edge. Meeting the family for the first time was not something that she particularly looked forward to. Despite her best intentions, she always felt like she talked too much and made a fool of herself. Doing her best to calm the quivery sensation in her belly, she followed Jackson into the next room.

It was the room she had glimpsed when they'd been standing out on the porch. The room smelled of fresh pine, a real Christmas tree standing in the corner of the room, so tall that the gorgeous white-gowned angel on top almost reached the ceiling. The lights twinkled merrily off glass ornaments of all shapes and sizes. Quinn's favorite ones that she could see looked like they'd been made by the children. She idly wondered if there were some a little boy Jackson had made. She became aware of a hush that had fallen over the room, expectant eyes glued to her.

"I'm sorry, I was just taken with the tree. We don't get live ones very often in Australia."

"What do you have then?" asked the boy who looked to be about nine years old.

"My family has a fake one with fiber optic lights through it." Quinn replied, smiling her thanks as the woman she assumed was Jackson's sister moved over to make space for her. Quinn sat down awkwardly with Duchess's pet carrier at her feet.

"Oh, reckon that would work too." Obviously, her answer was acceptable, and he focused on the board game again.

"I'm Beth, Jackson's sister." The blonde woman had the same coloring as both Jackson and his father but with Hannah's features. "This is my husband, Levi, you've just met Jimmy, and that's his sister, Laura. Pop and Grandma would've liked to be here, but Pop has been a little under the weather, and Grandma insisted he go to bed. I'm sure you'll meet them both tomorrow." Quinn politely smiled and nodded at everyone.

"Here you go, Quinn. Now, I hope you like marshmallows. I've taken the liberty of putting some in for you." Hannah bustled in, steaming mug in hand.

"Is there any other way to have hot cocoa?" Quinn asked.

"Don't reckon there is," Jimmy said. "What you got in the container?" He thrust his chin in the direction in question.

"Is it okay if I let her out now? She could really do with having a stretch, and I packed a tray and some kitty litter for her too," Quinn asked Hannah.

"Of course. You can set her litter tray up in the laundry."

Jackson stood. "I can do that while you help get her comfortable with everyone."

Jimmy looked like he was in danger of falling off his seat as he leaned forward, trying to get a glimpse of what was inside. Quinn knelt down and opened the door to the carrier.

"Hey, mama, time to get out and meet everyone." Disgruntled silence greeted her. "Now Duchess, everyone will think you're being very rude."

Nitro, his eyes unblinking, had slinked forward, his nose twitching to get a smell of the new house guest. Suddenly, he spun around and scampered out of the room only to return seconds later with an old plush teddy in his mouth. Gently, his whole body wiggling and wagging in his eagerness to please this being, he place it down, for all the world looking like a worshiper at an altar for some cat pagan goddess. Slowly, inch by inch, Duchess emerged.

"Oh, isn't she, like, the cutest thing you've ever seen?" squealed Laura.

Duchess didn't bother to glance in her admirer's direction. Once fully emerged, she gave a languid stretch and made her way to a dog bed that had been set up close to the crackling fireplace. She haughtily sniffed it before delicately, paw by paw, making her way onto it. With a final sniff, she set herself down, her belly extended. Safely ensconced on her throne, she ignored her captivated audience and began to wash herself. Nitro, whose bed Quinn was pretty sure Duchess had just stolen, settled down with his front paws touching the edge of the bed and rested his head on them, staring adoringly at the new center of his universe.

Quinn laughed at the animals' interactions. "Wow, Duchess, why don't you make yourself at home."

Laura and Jimmy had crept closer. "She looks a bit fat," Jimmy said. Duchess fixed a golden eye on him, letting her critic know of her displeasure.

"Jimmy, how can you say that? She's gorgeous." Laura loyally defended the pregnant queen.

Jackson, catching the end of the conversation after setting Duchess's facilities up in the laundry, laughed. "Jimmy, my boy, a word to the wise. That is not a cat you want to get on the wrong side of. And she's pregnant."

"Really?" squealed Laura, clapping her hands together. "Is she going to have them while you are here?"

"We don't actually know when she's due. The vet can only guess because she was given up for adoption," Quinn said, scooping Duchess up. "I'd better make sure she knows where the tray is. We don't want any accidents."

"I'll show you where I put it," Jackson gallantly offered. As she followed him, the heavy weight of Duchess in her arms, Nitro's nails clinked on the floorboards behind them. A warmth infused her. She didn't know why she'd been so worried. His family was just like him—normal, decent folk. Quinn crossed her fingers, hidden by Duchess's long fur. Maybe this was going to be a Christmas to remember after all.

CHAPTER 17

The weight of the blankets and duvet pressed comfortingly down on Quinn. Duchess snored softly, curled up at the back of Quinn's neck where she'd made herself a nest in the covers Quinn had pulled up around her head. Drowsily, she looked around what had once been Beth's old room. The heavy drapes were a floral pattern of purple and pink set against a beige background, the wallpaper a pink tone with stripes. There was something cozy and warm about the room. She could imagine a young Beth curled up here, maybe Jackson coming in and teasing her.

And just like that, Jackson filled her senses. She had been unbelievably nervous about meeting his family. It was funny, she hadn't met Lance's family once the entire time they'd dated, but here she was spending Christmas with the kin of a man she'd only spent a few weeks with over the entire year. Quinn had been blown away with how welcoming they'd been last night. They were good people.

Excruciating pressure on her bladder could not be ignored, no matter how snug the nest. That is, if she didn't want to have to explain an embarrassing accident, she'd better get up pronto. With a groan, she threw back the covers and hastily wrapped her dressing gown around her shivering body, the tremors adding to her urgency. Her feet curled up in protest as she thrust them into icy slippers before dashing across the hall, almost in tears.

Quinn sighed in relief as the pressure eased. Washing her hands, she noticed a bottle of aftershave on the counter. *Trust Jackson to not have some fancy designer aftershave. This looks like something he picked up from the drugstore.* Quinn brought the bottle to her nose and breathed in the fragrance. Something wasn't quite right. Sure, it was mostly how Jackson smelled whenever she was near him, but it was missing something, some tiny note of complexity. A quivery jolt went through Quinn when she realized the missing piece of the puzzle was Jackson himself. The musky tone was something unique just to him.

Feeling rather chuffed with herself, she opened the door. *Oh my goodness, is that?* Her nose began to twitch as she breathed in deeply. Yep, there it was. The unmistakable aroma of bacon. Feet barely touching the ground, she let the delectable temptation lead her into the kitchen. Standing at the stove, sizzling fry pan full of bacon in front of her, was Hannah.

Last night, Jackson's mother had been kind and welcoming, but this morning it felt like a fresh start—a nervous one at that without Jackson there for support. Hannah was already dressed for the day in jeans and a sweater, her hair scraped back into a no-nonsense ponytail. Guilty, Quinn looked down at her own pajamas and robe, complete with her pink fuzzy sleepers. *She's gonna think I'm a bloody layabout coming down here in my pajamas.* Awkwardly, Quinn stood at the threshold of the kitchen neither completely in nor out.

"Morning, Quinn. How did you sleep?" Hannah sent her a

warm smile, although she did sweep a quick gaze over her attire. "The boys are out doing the livestock, but they'll be back in for breakfast. Now, pull up a chair. Would you like some coffee?"

Quinn sheepishly sunk down. "I slept really well, thank you. I actually don't drink coffee. Maybe one day when I grow up." *I hope she doesn't think I'm a spoiled princess.* "Is there something I can help with?"

"How 'bout you set the table? Everything you need is in the drawer and cupboard over there." Hannah pointed in the direction behind Quinn with the spatula.

Quinn quickly set to work, feeling better now that she had a job to do, even if she was still in her nightwear. "I'm usually still asleep," she admitted.

"Round here, you don't get much of a lie in. If the sun's up, so are we—and usually before it, most of the time. But I imagine you keep different hours to us."

"Most of the time, yes. It's the nature of the job." Quinn fidgeted with the last fork that she was laying on the table, turning it over in her hands. She wasn't sure if she was being judged and somehow found wanting or if she was just being insecure.

"Have you always worked in casinos?" The sizzling increased as Hannah turned the bacon expertly over.

Quinn's stomach grumbled, protesting at not being able to attack the delicious crispy strips of yum immediately. Forcing herself to concentrate on what the older woman was saying to her, she shook her head. "No, this is my first time being a hostess. Back home, I was a PR assistant and some of the time I still am, when I don't have a high roller to look after."

"Oh, so how did you end up in Las Vegas?" Hannah peered at her curiously.

"Well, I worked with my friend back home and when she got a job over here, she arranged it so that I could come, too." Quinn didn't think Jackson's mom had to know about the horror ex-boyfriend she'd had to escape either.

"Sounds like a good friend. So your family is back in Australia? Do you think you'll stay in America for a while, or are you planning on going back?"

Is she interrogating me? I mean, if she is, she's doing it in the nicest possible way. "I don't have any immediate plans to go home. I mean, I was missing my family a while back, especially coming into Christmas. Nothing felt like it should. And then I met Jackson again and he invited me here." Her voice trailed off. Quinn wasn't sure she was ready, no matter how nice Jackson's mom was, to completely spill just how much it had meant to her.

"I can tell he cares about you. I can't rightly think of another time that he's ever brought a girl home for Christmas. I knew you must be something special when he told me he was bringing you, and I was right." Calmly, Hannah began to serve the bacon up, adding thick slabs of toast slathered in butter, completely oblivious to the stunned silence of the other woman.

Woah, Jackson's never brought a girl home. Why is this the first I've heard about it? Quinn stood, caught off guard at Hannah's admission. A fluttering in her belly left her feeling giddy and lightheaded, her breath bottling up in her throat. If Quinn was being honest, she didn't think Jackson was the kind of guy who would bring women home all the time—especially for Christmas—but she'd still assumed that he had at least once or twice. Right on cue, Jackson and his father came in, stamping the snow off their boots at the back door as they shrugged out of their jackets.

Acting like it was the most natural thing in the world,

Jackson leaned over and gave her a kiss where she sat. "Morning, how'd you sleep?"

Caught in the maelstrom of emotions she dropped her gaze. "Good morning, I slept fine. Duchess is still snuggled up in bed." Was it wrong how the little act of domesticity twisted her heart like a glimpse of what she could have? *What happens when this fantasy ends and we both go back to our real lives?* "Your mom said you were out checking on the animals."

"Yeah, this time of year, we need to feed them twice a day." Jackson took his place beside her, Hannah putting steaming plates of bacon and eggs in front of the men and returning with her own and Quinn's. Both men dug into the plates of food in front of them. *I guess working on a ranch gives a man a healthy appetite.* "If you like, after breakfast, I can give you a tour of the ranch. You didn't really get a chance to see much last night."

"I'd love to."

"You better put something warmer on first." Hannah smiled at her over her steaming coffee cup. "Even Texas Gore-Tex would be better."

"I don't think I packed any of that." Quinn felt silly for not being prepared.

Jackson laughed and gave his mother a warning look. "Mom, leave her alone." He rested his arm on the back of Quinn's chair. "Texas Gore-Tex isn't something you would have. She was teasing, but you still might want to get changed first."

Quinn's face burned under the teasing. Feeling foolish, she nodded and concentrated on her food. *Tomorrow, I'm going to set my alarm.*

～

SNUGGLY RUGGED up in the brand new Canadian goose coat she'd bought just for this visit, Quinn sat beside Jackson in his truck as he drove her around the ranch. He'd started the tour in one of the red barns, proudly leading her through the tall double doors. Inside, her searching eyes were greeted by rough wooden walls and animal stalls, straw scattered across the floor. Spider webs clung to corners like delicate lace, gently fluttering in the breeze. Quinn breathed in deeply. A comforting mix of straw, grain and wood mingled with the smell of animal urine and manure. Somehow, she half expected Lassie to come trotting out from a corner. As it was, Nitro was enthusiastically chasing some sort of vermin in one of the stalls.

Jackson's face was tight as he glanced around. "It needs a bit of work, but it's been standing since my pop built it." Quinn was taken aback by the defensive tone in Jackson voice.

"I think it looks cute."

He looked like he didn't believe her. *Maybe it's an insult to call a man's barn cute?* Quinn wasn't really sure what the etiquette for barns was. She didn't have a chance to ponder it further before he was ushering her back out into the bracingly cold air. Thankfully, it was only for a moment before she was safely inside the warm truck.

Now she sat as he drove her down muddy laneways between snow-covered paddocks, cattle idly staring at them from the distance where they stood in groups eating. Rows upon rows of fencing stretched out into the distance. Jackson described how many heads of stock were in each field, the breed, even how many acres. He glowed with love for each and every animal. She was fairly sure it extended right down to the blades of grass that were dormant under the blanket of snow. He belonged to this land in a way she'd never felt about anywhere or, until now, anyone.

The truck pulled to a halt on top of a rise overlooking the ranch. From this angle, the breath-taking vista looked like a neatly set out patchwork blanket in shades of white, cream and gray, the fencelines providing the little squares and rectangles. The cluster of houses each had wisps of smoke coming from the chimneys. In fact, Quinn realized with a start that this was the first Christmas she'd ever spent with an actual legitimate chimney for Santa to climb down on Christmas Eve.

"It's beautiful. I can see why you were so eager to get home for this last year." Quinn's breath sent steam dancing into the air.

"This is my favorite spot on the entire ranch. When I was growing up, if Mom or Dad ever needed to find me if I was slacking off, they knew to come look for me here." Quinn pictured a young Jackson, all long limbs, knobby knees, and not quite enough muscle on bone to cover it. "One day, this is where my kids are going to grow up."

Jackson's eyes met hers, his gaze so deep and intense that Quinn's heart fluttered, her stomach tying itself up in knots. "You want kids soon?" Of course he did. She'd seen how much his family meant to him.

"Yeah." He regarded her steadily with his piercing blue eyes and she found she couldn't look away. "I want to retire from the circuit. I was planning on doing one more year, but my heart just isn't in it anymore. It wants something else now." He cleared his throat, finally breaking eye contact and staring out over the land again. "So, I aim to build myself a house. Right here."

"I can picture it now." Quinn held her hands up, framing the space with her fingers. "House here, a garden here. Would you have a hen house?"

"Definitely."

She took a few steps to one side and pointed down at the snow. "Then the hen house would be here."

"Is that so?" He quirked a brow at her. "Seems to me I need you around to help with building this house."

Her mouth went dry, opening and closing several times. *Bloody heck, Quinn. Say something. He's going to think you're a right idiot if you stand here catching flies—or snowflakes.* He smiled at her, not quite reaching his eyes. Eyes that now looked sad. A knot formed in her stomach that she'd managed to ruin the mood.

"Have you ever built a snowman?"

"No."

He bent down and began to roll snow into a ball between his hands. "Well, I think it's about time we fixed that." Without warning, he threw the ball of snow at her. "Beginning with the traditional pre-snowman-building snow fight."

Laughing, she dodged nimbly out of the way, trying to scoop up some snow as he charged her. Retaliating, she threw her hastily compacted ball at him and fled as another snowball came flying her way. She squealed and ducked, but not fast enough this time and it hit the side of her hat, knocking it off into the snow.

"Here, let me get that for you."

Too late, Quinn realized it was all a ruse, and once his long strides had eaten up the distance between them, his hand snaked out to capture her as he washed her face with the snow he'd craftily hidden in his hand behind his back, all while she hollered and giggled and wiggled, trying to escape from his hold.

Breathless, she looked up at him, her vision slightly blurred by the snow that clung to her lashes. "Does this mean I'm ready to make a snowman, or have you just made me into one?"

"Nearly. There's one last thing I need to do."

She lifted an eyebrow, trying unsuccessfully to trap her smile before it blossomed over her face. "And what's that?"

Jackson put a gloved hand, now chilly and damp from the snow, under her chin, lifting it. "This." Then his lips were there, warm against hers, the chill of the snow fight fleeing before the heat of his kiss.

Now this was how a girl should keep warm.

QUINN SAT cross-legged on the floor, Duchess draped partially over her lap and getting maximum benefit from both her owner's body warmth and the heat of the crackling fire. Nitro was lying with his back butted up against the cat's, and Jackson wasn't entirely sure who the dog wanted contact with the most—Quinn or Duchess. He watched as she engaged in a very animated game of dominos with Laura and Jimmy. Beth was asking her about some of the craziest requests she'd had from people, and everyone was laughing at what she was revealing. Strange how natural it felt to have her here, sitting with his family as though she'd always been a part of the puzzle. And his family liked her. He could tell by how Jimmy followed her around and Laura had started using some of her Aussie slang. Heck, Grandma, now that Pop was feeling better, had already offered to give Quinn one of her closely-guarded recipes.

Worry wormed its way into his soul, twisting and churning in his gut. He'd seen the life she was leading in Vegas—bright lights, fancy cars, men with so much money they could blow more on an evening than he made in a whole year. Heck, he knew how much she loved her fashion and looking pretty. Not that he was complaining. He loved looking at her. But would she really like the life of living on the ranch? Frankly, he wasn't sure if she'd be willing to give up her high heels.

Even the things they did here for fun didn't compare. Tomorrow, everyone was heading into town to watch the lights get turned on at the Christmas Tree in the town square. It was nothing like the blazing piece of over-the-top foliage she'd shown him on The Strip.

"Does anyone want some eggnog?" his mom asked and, receiving several affirmative answers, headed into the kitchen.

Jackson padded on sock clad feet after her. "Need help, Mom?"

"No, but you can tell me what's bothering you." Hannah gave him a sharp look. He'd never been able to get anything past her. "If it helps, I can see how much you care about her, and I like her, too. I'd be proud to have her as my daughter-in-law. You and her would have beautiful babies together."

Jackson didn't want to admit even to himself how appealing the thought of Quinn, swollen with his child in her belly, was to him. "I think you're getting a bit ahead of yourself, Mom. I don't know if this is the life that Quinn wants."

Hannah ladled eggnog into some cups, wiping the liquid she'd dribbled over the sides off before setting them down on the counter. She licked her fingers, eyes sympathetic as she gazed at her son. "I was listening to her stories and she has a pretty exciting life—very different from how we live here on the ranch. But the girl I see out there, well, I think there's more to her than you give her credit for. Sure, she seems like a city girl, and a big city girl at that, but I think if you scratch under the surface a bit, you might just find a bit of country." Hannah handed him a mug of eggnog and patted him understandingly on the back.

Jackson mulled over her words as he sipped, the velvety creaminess comforting as the bourbon left a trail of warmth on its way down his throat. Outside he could see Quinn laughing at something his grandad had said to her, eyes glowing and cheeks flushed from the heat of the fire. *And maybe her enjoyment of the company.* Jackson silently mulled his mother's words over. *But was that enough to make up for what he would ask her to give up?*

CHAPTER 18

*M*aybe Mom's right, Jackson decided. *But I'm not sure if Quinn's going to enjoy getting down and dirty for me to find out.* It was time for her to be exposed to what life on the ranch was really like, and helping with his chores around the ranch was a great place to start. He did feel a little bad when her pristine fancy coat began to get a coating of fine chaff dust and stalks of hay as she sat on the back of his truck, throwing off slabs of feed to the stock. Watching her rosy cheeks and red nose from the cold, it was hard not to get caught up in her infectious smile. *Dang it, but he was proud of his girl.* His heart clenched as he caught himself. His girl. Was she? Or was she just his for now, somehow being loaned to him and soon to be snatched away, back to her castle overlooking the bright city lights?

She tapped on the glass to let him know that she'd thrown it all out and he pulled to a stop, letting her climb back into the warmth of the cab. "What's next, boss?" Her eyes sparkled mischievously.

"I need to split up some of the dry heifers from those that have calves at foot."

Quinn nodded sagely, her mouth pursed thoughtfully. Jackson felt his mouth quirk. *She has absolutely no idea what I'm talking about.* But he gave her full marks for throwing herself completely into the experience of being a ranch hand for the day. His mother's words echoed in his ear, and Jackson found himself praying for a Christmas miracle that she might be right. He pulled up at the cattle yards and grabbed his hat off the dash, door groaning as he swung it open. Quinn quickly met him at the front of the truck, squinting at the cattle milling around. Jackson half expected her to spit out a wad of tobacco with the show of grizzled experience she was pulling.

"You'll have to tell me what you need me to do," she said, feet firmly planted in the mud.

"I'm going to herd them toward where you'll be standing at the gate. All you have to do is swing it one way or the other depending on if the heifer has a calf or not."

"Sounds easy enough."

Once Quinn was in position, they set to work. Jackson waving and hollering, Nitro nipping at heels, driving them toward her. Quinn's face was scrunched up in concentration as she swung the gate as they came through. When the final calf trotted meekly by, she jumped down, smiling broadly at a job well done. Out of the corner of his eye, Jackson could see a lone cow charging toward her, obviously hot on the heels of her calf that had already gone through.

Quinn's eyes widened in alarm at the prospect of finding herself between the mama cow and her baby. Shrieking, she ran toward the gate and, with a display of athleticism that was truly awe-inspiring, cleared it with enough height that would have put a high jumper to shame. Unfortunately for her, her landing skills were sadly lacking, and she landed bum first in a muddy puddle on the other side. Judging from the squeals, it was a particularly cold one.

Jackson gallantly went to her aid, slightly marred by his wheezing breathing as he battled to contain his mirth. By the time he reached her, she'd already escaped from her unexpected mud bath and was standing with her dripping arms held away from her body. Not a single part of her wasn't drenched in thick, gloopy mud. Jackson wrinkled his nose at the rather uninviting aroma of manure and decaying straw wafting from her. Huge eyes were made bigger by the contrast of the whites of her eye against the dark splatter pattern on her face as she stared up at him. The corner of her mouth began to twitch, and she glanced down, surveying the havoc her hasty escape had wreaked on her appearance.

"I have no words." A hiccupping giggle escaped her.

"I don't, um." Jackson was lost to great gales of laughter. Quinn gave him a disgusted look before losing her own battle and joining him. Gasping for air and holding his sides, he struggled for control. Quinn's lips were turning blue and her teeth were chattering, even as she giggled. Remorse hit him like an icy shower. *She's soaking wet and cold.* Fierce pride blazed from him. *And not one word of complaint from her.* "Miss, I think we need to get you back to the ranch ASAP and into a nice hot shower."

Quinn gave a little sniff. "A hot shower sounds divine. And plenty of soap will be in order, too."

Jackson was still angrily remonstrating himself when he ushered her into the house, helping divest her of her muddy coat, hat, gloves and boots. *Good lord, but she reeks.* Hannah took one look at her pinched, frozen face and herded her up toward the bathroom with promises of a nice cup of hot cocoa to warm her up when she finished.

"My word, what did you do to that poor girl?"

"Well, I did what you suggested. I went looking to find the country girl in Quinn." Jackson couldn't quite meet his mother's incredulous stare. "Now that I think about it, the state she's in—it's actually your fault."

"I said scratch the surface, not throw her into a mud pile."

He winced at the strident tone in his mother's appalled voice. "To be fair, she leapt into the puddle all by herself."

"You'd have me believe she ended up like that and you had absolutely nothing to do with it?"

"Well, the heifer chasing her might've helped."

"You let a heifer chase her?" Jackson hadn't heard that particular high-pitched screech since he was a teenager and had tied fireworks to the cat's tail. He wasn't quite sure if his mom was going to slap him or not. Judging from her expression, she hadn't made up her mind either.

"You should have seen her clear the gate. She did it in a single jump, barely touched it. The puddle on the other side was where things went a little awry." *Dang, but the girl had moved fast.*

Hannah sighed heavily, obviously at a loss for words, and began to make cocoa. Now that the hilarity of the situation had passed, he began to fidget, digging some caked-on mud out from under his fingernails. *Dang it, Jackson, you might just as well have shoved her face-first into the nearest pile of manure. Ain't no way she'll want this over the luxury of her normal life.* An ache built in the back of his throat and his chest felt heavy as he contemplated what had just occurred. *What if, by trying to show her what my life is like and what I can offer her, I've only succeeded in driving her away?*

Light footsteps announced her imminent arrival. He gaped at her choice in fashion, *What the heck? Did her luggage get mixed up?* Sure, the jeans were tight-fitting and suited her, but her choice in sweater was so outlandish there was no way she actually owned it. Jackson pressed his lips tightly together, battling the irony of her choice. Black and white cowhide pattern covered the sleeves, and a closer inspection revealed the splotches were actually bells, Christmas trees, doves and stars. But the pièce de résistance set against a background of green and red stars, a Santa hat jauntily on its head and festive scarf around its neck, stared out a large bovine face. Even Duchess stopped eating cat kibble under the watchful eye of Nitro to look askance at her owner.

Quinn, aware all eyes were on her, did a slow spin, apparently so they could take her sweater in in all its festive glory. "Pretty awesome, right? I thought it was pretty fitting after the day I've had." *How is it she can look so adorable in such an ugly sweater?*

"I don't think I've ever seen one quite like that," Hannah hedged, handing a mug of cocoa to her, sipping from the only other one she'd made. Jackson realized she hadn't made anything for him. *Mom isn't upset with me at all*, he thought sarcastically.

"When I saw this online after Jackson invited me here, I knew I had to have it. Christmas sweaters aren't really a big thing in Australia. It's more bikinis and thongs this time of year."

Hannah began to choke on her cocoa, and Jackson's mouth went dry, his mind going into dangerous territory as he pictured Quinn's normal festive attire. Quinn, for her part, scrunched up her face in confusion at their reactions. Sudden understanding dawned across her face and red crept steadily up her neck, blossoming on her cheeks. "No, no. Thongs as in flip flops, not what you're obviously thinking."

"Oh, I was beginning to think your family celebrated Christmas very differently from how we do." Hannah chuckled as she took another sip of her steaming drink.

"I didn't have a problem with it." Jackson loved watching Quinn squirm on the other end of his hot gaze.

"Jackson." Quinn's eyes were wide in outrage.

"Ignore him," Hannah admonished. "I think it's perfect for tonight."

Quinn beamed at her. "So do I."

Jackson, giving up on getting a cocoa, stood and began to make his own drink. *I think the other outfit sounded better...*

CAROLERS SANG like their hearts would explode with joy for the newborn Christ as Quinn promenaded with Jackson under the festively lit trees of the park. The entire family had come into town tonight, including Pop and Grandma, to watch the turning on of the town's Christmas Tree set up in the square. Rugged up in a fresh spare coat she'd had the forethought to pack, Quinn was a little disappointed that no one would get to see her snazzy sweater.

"Hurry up, we're gonna miss it." Jimmy jumped up and down on the spot, urging them on with his hands.

"Settle down, young man," Grandma admonished. "Pop and I aren't getting any younger. Anyhow, they ain't gonna start without us there."

Quinn smiled. The Gregory Clan was out in force tonight, and she felt completely at home with them. "Are you warm enough?" Jackson bent down solicitously to her.

He probably feels bad about laughing at me earlier, and so he should. My sweater is spectacular. She shrugged deeper into her coat, the scarf pulled high around her ears, gloved hands shoved deep into her pockets. "Nice and toasty, thank you."

"Let me know if you get cold. I'll make sure to keep you warm." A delicious thrill danced up her spine at the mischievous grin pinned to his mouth.

"I'll keep that in mind."

"Jackson!" a man hollered over the crowd.

A broad smile broke out over Jackson's face when he spotted the owner of the voice. "Wyatt, I thought you weren't going to make it tonight." The two men hugged, thumping each other on the back with gloved hands.

"Well, you know me. I can't let you have all the pretty ladies to yourself." The black-haired man winked at Quinn, his smile infectious. She found herself grinning back at him.

"Wyatt, this is Quinn. Quinn, this is my best friend, Wyatt." Jackson's arm slipped easily around her waist, pulling her in close. There was something vaguely possessive about the gesture. It didn't escape Wyatt either, given the speculative twinkle in his eyes.

"Pleased to meet you, Quinn."

"Likewise, Wyatt."

"Now, I want to know how this ugly, beaten-up old cowboy managed to get a girl like you, and where can I get one?" Wyatt flirted.

Quinn laughed easily. "Well, he had to go all the way to Australia to find one that would have him, and it just so happens that you're in luck. I brought a friend back over with me."

Wyatt made a show of looking around. "Where is she?"

"Unfortunately for you, she should be almost in Bora Bora by now."

"Expensive tastes," Wyatt noted.

"You have no idea," muttered Jackson. "We better catch up with the rest of the family. I wouldn't want Quinn to miss the lights."

Wyatt grinned at his friend, getting the not-so-subtle hint. "It was nice to meet you. I hope it won't be the last." With a final teasing smirk to his friend, Wyatt made his way back through the crowd in the direction he'd come from.

"He seemed nice," Quinn said as they made their way forward again.

"Yeah, he's a good guy. I've known him since elementary school." Jackson still hadn't removed his arm from around her. *I could get used to this side of Jackson. Who would have thought he'd be so possessive in front of his friends?* Quinn basked in a warm glow of security.

They finally caught up with the rest of the family just as the countdown began for the tree to be lit up. Quinn found herself caught up in the excitement, giddily clapping her hands, and then the tree exploded into a blaze of light. Her breath caught at the spectacle, the shining star on top so bright it could have joined the real ones twinkling above.

"If you like, we can leave the rest of the family here and go for a walk?" Jackson's breath was warm against her ear.

"I'd like that."

Quietly, they slipped away, making their way through the press of people. An ice-skating rink had been set up, people gliding silently across the softly glowing surface casting long shadows. Trees framing the rink were lit from below, their pale slender limbs stretching toward the heavens as if in homage. Snowflakes gently began to fall.

"It's like something out of a movie." Her breath created frosty puffs of steam as she spoke. "It's so different from any Christmas I've ever had back in Australia. This is so magical. The whole time I've been here has been like a dream."

"Even being chased by a cow?" His eyes crinkled as he grinned at her.

"Even then. I was beginning to think I'd lost my Christmas spirit, but being here with you, with your family, the ranch. You have no idea the gift you've given me."

"I'd give you everything I had if you asked for it." Snowflakes were beginning to cling to his eyelashes, settling on his broad shoulders. *He's the perfect image of a Christmas cowboy*. Quinn couldn't resist standing on her tiptoes and kissed him, his nose cold against hers, but his mouth hot and demanding. She didn't know if there was an explanation for her feelings for him, but she couldn't escape it. She might just be falling in love with this humble cowboy.

CHAPTER 19

Quinn had a smudge of confectioner's sugar on her nose as she laughed with his mom, Beth, Laura, Jimmy and Grandma. She looked to be in her element, having spent most of the Christmas Eve day in the kitchen with the womenfolk of his family, chatting, giggling and managing to find time to make a gingerbread house and Christmas decorated sugar cookies. Jackson, watching her, now knew the torment of being in love. He railed against the injustice to give him a glimpse of what his soul longed for and not let him keep it.

Quinn, tongue poking slightly out of her mouth in concentration, carefully cradled a snowflake cookie in her hand as she softly padded over to him. "This one I did especially for you, and considering I've spent a lot of time with a French-trained pastry chef, you should be honored."

Like a kid who had just offered the best marble from their collection, she stood, face hopefully expectant for his opinion. Jackson looked down at her confectionery masterpiece. In the center, she'd written *QW 4 JG* in bold red lettering.

Jackson's heart twisted at her earnest expression, eyes glowing with her feelings for him. Feelings that pulled him in and knotted him up.

Was it possible that what she felt was more than just a holiday fling, that it was deeper than that? He opened his mouth to say that JG loved QW too, but crushing fear smothered the words before they could form. Instead he gave a small smile of thanks.

"You did a great job of decorating it. Doubt I could do half as good." *Coward.* Quickly, he turned away, but not before he caught a glimpse of bewilderment flash across her previously happy face. *A coward and a jerk.*

"Everyone"—Grandma clapped her hands together for attention—"I think it's time to clean up, then it's time to hang the stockings."

Jackson took the opportunity to escape to the living room, joining his father, Pop and Levi. "The women are almost done by the sounds of it," Pop said.

"Yep," Jackson said, sitting beside him.

"Reckon your mom will want me to go and bring the Christmas stockings down," Jackson's dad said, rising to his feet and setting about his business.

Before long, he'd returned, and the rest of the family had gathered in front of the fireplace, ready for the Gregory Christmas Eve tradition of hanging the Christmas stockings. Grandma stepped forward with Pop, and together they hung the first stocking. It was blank and was placed with care for all the Gregory's who were gone but not forgotten on this most special of holy nights. Pop's hand rested a moment, lingering over some unseen memory that made his hazy eyes damp. Next, they each hung their own before returning to their seats. Jackson's dad and mom were next, followed by Levi, Beth and their children.

If I don't do this now, I'm never going to. Jackson stood to take his turn, clearing his throat. "Just before I do mine, I need to go get something." He stepped out, quickly gathering what he was after and returned. Picking up his stocking, he hung it beside the rest of his family. "There's just one thing missing. Pop, if you will do the honors for me." The old man stood, enjoying all eyes on him in surprise, and pulled a hammer and nail out from where he'd stashed them earlier on the mantlepiece in readiness. Gnarled fingers made deft work, and with a wink at his grandson, he sat down again.

Jackson pulled the green and yellow stocking out from beneath his sweater, his finger tenderly tracing the name spelled out in diamantes. *Gosh, I hope she understands what I'm saying.* Hanging it, he gave it a critical look before stepping back to reveal it.

"I think that's much better."

Quinn's hand flew to her mouth, her eyes shimmering with unshed tears. "You really got me my own Christmas stocking?"

Jackson nodded, giving a grunt of surprise as she leapt off the sofa to throw herself into his arms. *Maybe I didn't need to worry, after all.* She smelled of ginger, cinnamon and nutmeg. The very essence of Christmas.

"Thank you so much. You have no idea what this means to me." She hiccupped.

"Looks like you're almost officially part of the family now." Hannah's voice was thick with emotion.

Jackson looked at Quinn, lost in her beautiful hazel eyes that spoke to his heart in a way he never knew possible. Darn it all. He loved her, and he was pretty sure she felt the same way. Maybe there was hope after all, because she sure as heck didn't look upset about becoming part of the family. In fact, she looked the polar opposite.

Grandma raised her glass of eggnog in toast. "A Christmas Eve wish. May you have the gladness of Christmas which is hope, the spirit of Christmas which is peace, and the heart of Christmas which is love."

Staring at the beautiful woman at his side, he prayed that his Christmas wish would come true.

QUINN'S HEART was overflowing as she lay in bed, her chest expanding, a wonderous sensation of acceptance seeping into every pore. The Gregory's liked her. They'd made it so very clear tonight. The harsh ring of her phone broke through her pleasant pondering. *What on earth is bloody Kelly doing calling me at this time of night?*

"Hi, Kelly. Aren't you supposed to be in Bora Bora?"

"I am, but my phone keeps blowing up with calls. You're never going to guess what's happened."

"They've run out of tequila?" Quinn looked under the covers, wondering where Duchess had gotten too.

"Ha-ha, very funny. Seems like you've really irritated Markus Jamison. Turns out, he's shown up at The Chimera expecting you to be waiting for him. When he found out that you weren't kidding about other plans for Christmas, well, I don't think he's going to take no for an answer."

"It's a bit late for that, Kelly. It's bloody Christmas Eve."

"I don't think he cares. He's demanding that you're there tomorrow at the latest or you won't have a job."

Shocked outrage coursed through Quinn's body. *Who did he bloody well think he was, making demands of her like that?* "Well, too bad. He's not my boss, and I don't have to listen to his threats."

"Um, that's the thing. Both Julie and Lachlan have called

me. Apparently, you were out of range or something. Anyway, turns out he is, and you do."

"What? You're not making any sense."

"Markus has bought The Chimera. He's now your—well, all of ours—boss." The air rushed out of Quinn's lungs in a great gush. She'd suspected Markus wasn't a man used to his desires being unfulfilled, but she didn't think he would go so far to actually buy an entire casino. "I mean, when you think about it, it's actually kinda flattering."

"You think a man trying to force a woman to go to another country for Christmas against her will is flattering?"

"Well, obviously not when you say it like that. But I've never had someone buy a casino to get me to go on a date with them. So, what are you going to do?"

Quinn was torn, conflicted by the harsh reality of needing the job and not wanting to leave Jackson. "I don't know," she whispered.

"Well, you better hurry up and figure it out. Anyway, my cocktail has arrived and I wouldn't want it to get hot. Give my love to Jackson." And with that, the line went dead.

Quinn cradled the phone in her hands, staring down at it. Jackson hadn't actually said anything about how he felt about her. Sometimes he would look at her or say something and she was sure that there was this connection between them, and other times, well, she wasn't so sure. Cold uncertainty settled hard and heavy in the pit of her stomach. *What if I'm wrong and he doesn't like me half as much as I like him?* Could she risk losing her job and home on a maybe?

Frustrated, she covered her head with her pillow. *Argh, why couldn't this be simple? Girl likes boy, boy likes girl, and they live happily ever after with a cat, dog and some kittens.* Quinn looked around her room, but there still was no sign of Duchess. It wasn't like the pampered pregnant feline to stray too far from comfort and heat these days. Worried, she decided to have a quick look to see if perhaps Duchess had commandeered Nitro's bed near the fire.

Quinn stopped, surprised, on the threshold of the living room. Jackson stood in the shadows cast by the flickering fire in front of her Christmas stocking. "Careful Santa doesn't see you." Quinn gave a chuckle when his large frame jerked in shock. *Oh my gosh, could he look any more guilty? Like a kid caught with his hand in the cookie jar.*

"What are you doing up and about this time of the night?" Jackson asked. *Well played. Distract by going on the offensive.*

"Kelly called, and now I can't find Duchess."

His brows drew together. "Kelly scared Duchess off when she called?"

"No, Kelly called to say the casino has sold and I need to get back there by tomorrow if I still want a job." Quinn waved her hand dismissively. "That's a whole other issue. I'm really starting to worry that I can't find Duchess."

Jackson looked worried, his eyes shadowed and unhappy. Quinn couldn't be sure which piece of news had caused it. "Now that you mention it, I haven't seen Nitro for a while. The last I saw him was when everyone was still here. I'm sure they can't be too far."

But no amount of searching revealed the missing canine and feline duo. *Please, please, please be all right, Duchess.*

"Look, maybe they managed to slip outside," Jackson said, admitting defeat.

"If something bad has happened to her, I'm never going to forgive myself." *Now's the time to jump out from wherever you're hiding, Duchess.*

"She's a Maine Coon. She's got some of the thickest fur I've ever seen on a cat to keep her warm."

"She's also a heavily pregnant lady." Quinn rushed to the back door. The snow that had only been gently falling when they'd said goodnight to the rest of the family earlier was now getting heavier. "I have to find her."

"Not without these you aren't." Jackson held out her coat and boots. "I know you're worried, but there is no way I'm letting you out there in nothing more than your pajamas."

"Fine," she huffed, hopping on one foot as she tried to put her boots on. Once she was suitably attired, she raised an eyebrow at Jackson. "Happy?"

"I'd be happier curled up in bed with a book, but here we are, about to traipse through the snow in search of a wayward pair of animals."

Quinn was thrown by the image he gave her. *I wonder what he's reading.* "Wait, you read in bed?"

"Of course I do. It's the only time of the day I get a chance to. Now, let's get going. The sooner we start looking out there, the sooner we can get back into a nice warm house." *And bed.*

The obvious place to start, according to Jackson, was the barns. The first one was empty and lifeless. The second, the faded red one he'd shown her on his tour, was beginning to seem the same when Quinn heard a whining noise. She stopped and put her finger to her lips, demanding silence so she could listen. There it was again, and with a rhythmic thumping. Stealthily so as not to frighten the would-be escapees, she crept on tiptoes to the stall closest to her. Inside, reflected back in the light of her torch were a pair of eerily glowing yellow eyes. Nitro!

Quinn flew to the dog's side, worried that he'd made no move to stand. In fact, except for his tail and happy face, he hadn't changed his position at all. She glanced over her shoulder at Jackson, fearful the dog was hurt and, if Nitro was wounded, where did that leave Duchess and in what condition?

As she knelt, she realized why the loyal dog had remained

in position. He was curled around Duchess, shielding her from the cold. Duchess, in turn, was wrapped around five mewling blind kittens. "Oh my, Duchess. You're a mom. But I don't think this is the best place to have your babies." She petted Nitro on the head. "Good boy, keeping them warm."

Jackson was already taking off his coat and ever so carefully, under the close watch of both Mama Cat and proud Uncle Dog, scooped the precious bundles into the toasty folds. "Let's get them all inside."

Quinn gently picked up Duchess, painfully conscious to not cause her cat any pain after having just given birth. It felt like an eternity to get them all back to the house and safely installed in Nitro's bed beside the fire. Duchess sniffed each kitten in turn, giving them a lick before wrapping her fluffy tail around her family like a furry comforter.

"Well, that was quite an adventure for Christmas Eve." Jackson smiled down to where an exhausted Duchess had closed her eyes, purring a lullaby to her kittens. Nitro dozed his head, resting on the edge of the bed.

Now that the excitement had passed, Quinn was beginning to feel the chill of where her pajamas had gotten wet. She was thankful that Jackson had insisted she at least put her coat on, or she would have been frozen into an icicle by now. "It certainly was. I'd better get changed into some dry pajamas."

"How about you do that, and I'll make us some hot cocoa to warm up?"

It took Quinn hardly any time to divest herself of her wet garments and put some dry ones on, her feet barely touching the floor as she made her way back to Jackson. He held out a steaming mug to her, which she gratefully accepted.

"You mentioned that Kelly said you had to be back in Vegas by tomorrow morning?"

"Yeah, but I don't want to go. Well, if you don't want me

to go?" Quinn looked at him. She felt exposed and vulnerable. *Please, Jackson, tell me not to go.* When he didn't respond, it felt like she'd been kicked in the guts. He wanted her to go. She was devastated that this was how their magical time together was ending.

"I'm scared that this thing we have isn't going to last." Quinn felt like Jackson had just taken a knife and twisted it into her heart. *What was he saying?* He raked his fingers agitatedly through his hair, blowing out his cheeks. "Heck, I'm just going to say it. If I don't, I reckon I'm gonna regret it for the rest of my life." Quinn stared at him, her heart in her mouth. "I know what I can give you isn't very exciting, but it's the only life I have to offer you."

"I thought it was plenty exciting getting chased by a cow."

His generous mouth quirked. "Yeah, well, I guess that was a little exciting."

Quinn placed her hand over his where it rested on his leg. "I've found a sense of belonging here that I didn't know I was missing in Vegas. I mean, I've made some great friends and, of course, Kelly is there. But it turns out the missing piece to me is here with you."

There was a light in his eyes, hopeful, but also primitive and possessive. The woman inside of her responded to the sheer male of him. "Does this mean you're not going back to the casino tomorrow?"

"You're not getting rid of me that easily. Not after I put so much effort into making those Christmas cookies. Plus, it would be a shame to break up the cat and dog." She gave his hand a squeeze, her throat constricting with her emotions.

"It sure would break their hearts." Jackson agreed.

Quinn nodded, her bottom lip quivering as she struggled to contain herself. "There's a lot to sort out, but this is where I want to be. That is, if you'll have me. I thought I'd lost my Christmas spirit, but maybe being out here on this ranch is where I needed to be to find it again. You and your family, you've reminded me of what Christmas is all about—being with your loved ones."

Blinking rapidly to stop the tears that threatened from spilling, she looked up and found, to her surprise, that they were both sitting under mistletoe. She could have sworn it hadn't been there earlier.

Jackson followed her gaze. "Well, if that isn't a sign." He looked back at her, his heart in his eyes. "I love you, Quinn."

A warm giddiness rushed through Quinn and she tried to swallow her heart back from her throat as his warm calloused hand gently cupped the side of her face. "I love you, too."

The fingers of his other hand loosely entwined with hers, and then he kissed her as if to breathe the very essence of Quinn into him. Outside the snow gently continued to fall silently to the ground as the clock inside struck midnight.

"Merry Christmas, Quinn," he whispered against her lips. "I don't know what I did to get on Santa's nice list, but I'm going to spend the rest of my life making sure I stay on it."

Quinn's mouth curved into a saucy grin. "Well, maybe once in a while it might be nice to be on the naughty list, too."

Somewhere in the distance she could have sworn she heard bells jingling, but under the mistletoe, she'd already received the best Christmas gift she could have ever hoped for.

True Love.

THE END

As an Indie Author, reviews help me get my books noticed. If you enjoyed reading Jackson's and Quinn's story as much as I

did writing it, please leave a review. It will make all the
difference to me.

If you loved, *Boots & Mistletoe,* sign up for my newsletter to
get exclusive bonus bits.

Now, turn the page as the Mistletoe Collection continues
with Kelly's story... *The Cowboy Under The Mistletoe*

CHRISTMAS DAY, BORA BORA

The turquoise waters were light panes of shimmering glass underneath azure-blue skies. Kelly tossed her phone onto the table beside her as she reclined back against her cabana, the sun-kissed fabric warm against her bikini clad body, and the balmy ocean breeze whispering across her tanned skin. Quinn could keep her freezing cold Colorado winter. Nothing said Christmas like an over-the-water bure in Bora Bora.

Twisting one of several delicate chains she wore around her neck and midriff, she languidly waved a hand in the air, signaling her need for the cute waiter. Tray in hand, he made his way over.

"Yes, miss?"

"I would like a Blue Hawaiian decorated with red and green cherries on a stick." *It was Christmas, after all.*

"Yes, miss."

Settling back down, she thought about Quinn again. It wouldn't surprise her if that girl ran off to the wild of freezing Colorado with her cowboy. Next thing everyone would know, she'd probably up and marry him. Markus

Jamison had severely underestimated that girl, and she was going to enjoy watching him stew over it at great length.

The waiter returned with her drink and a shot of tequila. Kelly looked up at him, confused. "I only ordered the cocktail."

"Yes, miss. The man sitting over there asked me to bring it to you."

Kelly lowered her glasses to get a better look at the fine specimen raising his glass at her in salute from the pool bar. *Merry Christmas to me.*

Kelly's story, *The Cowboy Under The Mistletoe*, is available for purchase on Amazon or free on Kindle Unlimited

ACKNOWLEDGMENTS

A debt of gratitude to my editor Rebekah Groves for her patience with me.

Another big thanks to Megan from Designed with Grace for her cover design.

To my amazing beta readers and street team, you guys rock and I couldn't do it without you. Special mention to Lisa and Cair.

And finally to my fabulous alpha reader Trixie Norman, for all the late nights of reading and endless question about your thoughts.

Have you read them all?

Cowboy Christmas Series

The Mistletoe Collection

Boots and Mistletoe

Cowboy boots, mistletoe, and a holiday do-over…

The Cowboy Under the Mistletoe

It'll take more than the magic of the season to help this grump find her happily ever after…

Mistletoe and the Billionaire's Cowgirl

In the barrels and hearts series

Available on Amazon and Kindle Unlimited

A bull rider's paradise

The prequel to the Barrels and Hearts series. True love is only the beginning….of the story. Find out where it all began with Ana and Eduardo. Sometimes finding love is easy. It's keeping it that's hard.

A cowgirl's dream

An Aussie cowgirl far from home. A handsome Brazilian bull rider. Can they have a rodeo love story of their dreams?

A cowgirl's heart

An Aussie cowgirl in need. Her childhood friend to the rescue. Can friendship turn into a love story?

A cowgirl's passion

One feisty cowgirl. One steadfast Brazilian bull rider. Will she see what is right in front of her?

A cowgirl's pride

An Aussie cowgirl from the wrong side of the tracks. A handsome equine vet. Can they find a way to have their happy ever after?

A cowgirl's love

A young Aussie cowgirl. A widowed rancher. Does age matter when it comes to love?

A cowgirl's movie star

A fiery cowgirl with big dreams. A movie star far from home. When their two worlds collide, will their love be strong enough to hold them together or will they be pulled apart

A cowgirl's billionaire

A cowgirl adrift. A broken billionaire cowboy. Can he free himself from the past to be the man she needs now?

Billionaire Hearts Ranch Series

February 2021 Release

The wounded cowboy billionaire

The cowboy's billionairess

The billionaire's cowgirl

The cowgirl's fake billionaire marriage

A cowboy's riches (Prequel)

ABOUT THE AUTHOR

Edith MacKenzie or Eddie Mac to her friends is an author of sweet and wholesome contemporary cowboy romance. They say in literary circles to write what you know, and Eddie has certainly taken that to heart. Before embarking on a writing career, she trained horses professionally and brings that wealth of knowledge to her writing.

Now a mum to a boy and girl, as well as wife, she delights with her tales of strong cowgirls and their adventures in finding love. When not weaving the love stories of her characters, she enjoys hanging out with her family and animals, as well as reading, fishing and camping.

Just remember—once a cowgirl, always a cowgirl.

facebook.com/EddieMacAuthor
amazon.com/Edith-MacKenzie
bookbub.com/profile/edith-mackenzie

www.ingramcontent.com/pod-product-compliance
Lightning Source LLC
Chambersburg PA
CBHW021156110726
47900CB00002B/599